FLY WITH THE FALCON

LOVE. LOSS. LIBERTY.

BY
ED COBLEIGH

DEDICATION

Dedicated to the women
who contributed to
this book

CHAPTER 1
MORRO BAY, CALIFORNIA

300 feet over the ocean, she pushed headfirst off the rock ledge and began falling unafraid into the void. After a long half-second, when clear of the wind-sculpted cliff face, she spread her broad wings, feeling the air. Stroking into the air rushing past her, she climbed. Blowing from offshore since before dawn, a stiff sea breeze pushed against the barrier cliff which diverted the airflow and shot the invisible current skyward. The updraft caught her, lifted her, hurled the bird to where she wanted to go.

Morro Rock, her aerie's location, wades in the shallow waters just offshore from California's Central Coast. The Pacific Ocean laps most of its circumference, seeking without success to erode the eternal volcanic stone. A broad, sandy causeway leads from the rock to the laid-back beach city of Morro Bay. Nearly six hundred feet tall and a quarter-mile wide, the rock is the plugged throat of an ancient volcano. Frozen in time and space, the hulking lava bubble stands guard over the entrance to a calm, protected harbor.

Composed of molten magma solidified eons ago, Morro Rock is sprinkled and crusted with bird excrement and other organic debris. Since time immemorial, the bird's direct ancestors have left their white-splashed streaks on the rock along with the desiccated remains of their once airborne prey. Dried guano and sun-bleached bones continue adding to Morro Rock's bulk to this day.

Ancients of the local Chumash indigenous people and countless generations of peregrine falcons have held the massive outcropping to be sacred ground. It is the source of their respective foundation myths. For years without number, both tribes, avian and human, have feasted, bred, mourned their dead, and worshiped the heavens on Morro Rock.

The rock's seaward face, hidden from the town, forced the west wind upward, an energy-saving vertical torrent offering a free boost to the azure sky for any flyers skilled enough to ride it. The bird rose ever higher with only the occasional beat of her outstretched wings. 500 feet, 750 feet, 1000 feet, until even Morro Rock's planform shrank beneath her. Eventually, the updraft faded. She circled, riding its last spent upwellings, at altitude, finally at home in the cool morning air. Her long, thin wingtip feathers flexed and tilted as her powerful wings pushed her forward, shoving flowing air downward and rearward. With the outline and the function of an oriental fan, her tail twisted left and right, shaping the airflow as it passed and left her. Each feather moved on its own in concert with its neighbors, keeping her coordinated with the slipstream. She lived and flew on the edge of disaster. Birds are aerodynamically unstable. Without her primary flight feathers constantly adjusting her flight path to keep her equilibrium, she would spin out of control. The falcon rode the airstream, balancing herself between the fluid forces providing her with life-sustaining lift and gravity's relentless pull.

Below, far below, squadrons of various birds squawked when she took wing, screeching out their respective species' unique danger cries. They warned others of their kind to the airborne predator's presence. White gulls glided, soaring as they watched fearfully above, their long, tapered wings generating effortless lift with little associated drag and with even less energy spent. Shorebirds wheeled, scattered across the foaming surf line and above the beige sand. Crows, inland corvids out for a day at the beach, cawed and circled, a thin, shifting *noir* cloud on the move as seen from the falcon's height.

In perfect, low-level V formation, a flight of gray pelicans coasted along, relatively unconcerned. They paralleled the curling wave tops, riding the slight air updrafts generated by the marching swells. Sturdy adult pelicans are too large to serve as a falcon's prey when easier kills appear available. The pelicans instinctively understood that dynamic.

Jet-black vultures with bald, blood-red heads also soared and glided, patiently awaiting the inevitable carrion they knew would come. Vultures cannot sustain flight by flapping, they must ride the updrafts, a skill at which they excel. Tiny ground squirrels scattered among the rocks outlining the causeway froze motionless, interpreting each birds' unique danger calls. Rodents rarely suffer predation by shoreline falcons, but it pays to be ultra-vigilant at the bottom of the food chain.

As she climbed into the sheltering sky, the peregrine gradually disappeared against the shinning-blue glare. She rose further into her atmospheric realm. The milling birds below relaxed, quieted down, and considered other vital birdie interests such as their next meal. Only the highly intelligent crows, with long memories, continued to watch for the unseen danger and to complain verbally about it. Death from above was now invisible to the most-likely prey birds, but still she was there, circling. Her coal-dark eyes, the binocular orbs of an apex predator, were much more acute than those of any potential kill. She saw them. They could not see her at all.

Peregrines are not pure soaring birds like the common red-tailed hawks or the hawks' more numerous cousins, the black vultures. While she rode the upwelling, her wings stayed mostly locked and motionless. Remaining at altitude required scant effort. Each wing thrust represented a few ergs of precious stored food energy lost. Updrafts generated by the rock made her flight nearly effortless. Without the vertical airflow, the longer she remained airborne, the more tiring her flight would become. A quick kill resulting in fast food represented her usual mission profile, but not today.

To fly for a peregrine is both a survival skill and a way of doing business. But sometimes when the wind blew just right, when the burning sun was not high, and when she had recently eaten, she flew for the unadulterated joy of it. The thrusting updraft brought her easily to her airborne orbit, throwing her into the sky. Enjoying the ride, she banked and turned, her wings occasionally fanning the air. It was a superb day to be a peregrine falcon.

Distant rolling thunder washed over her in-flight revelry, echoing off the rock and reverberating across the nearby town. The rumblings emanated from a cloudless sky, but few humans or birds noticed, each accustomed to the almost daily noise. Far above the falcon, two

United States Navy F/A-18 Super Hornet fighter jets streaked over the coast headed out to sea for a routine training sortie. The flight leader, once over water, signaled to her wingman to increase the howling engines' power level, producing even more thunderous clamor. The female fighter pilot epitomized the equal opportunities offered by aviation, whether conducted by bird or human. However, some flyers are considered more equal than others in both domains. Such distinctions were lost on the avian realm just above the earth's surface.

Far below, 50 feet over the paved sand spit leading to the town, flew a gaggle of ringed-neck doves, a non-native species. The disorganized swarm of flapping feathers made surprising speed. A singleton lagged behind the group, not quite able to keep up with its mates. Doves are fast flyers, but this one was not, its wings oddly uncoordinated and awkward.

Brief aerial playtime over, she looked earthward. Her gaze focused on the trailing bird. She locked her vision on her desired prey, ignoring the swirl of non-targeted birds beneath her. Banking out of her oval flight pattern, she turned away from the ocean and toward the shore. Her wings tilted just so, one pointed slightly to the sky, one shaded down toward the earth. Slowly, carefully, she matched her path with the flock of doves below, stalking them. Following their path from behind and from far above, out of sight, she adjusted her course putting the rising sun directly behind her. When she attacked, the flock would have to look back into old Sol's blinding glare.

Yes, that slower bird was the one. It looked unwell. She half-rolled onto her left side, wings partially folded against her body spilling their lift. Her feet and razor-sharp talons remained tucked tightly rearward, reducing parasitic wind drag. Her pale-yellow, hooked beak fell well below the hazy horizon as she fell into a nearly vertical dive. She reversed her roll back upright while keeping her wings closed in a perfect low-drag, teardrop profile. Falling initially under light gravity, she accelerated faster and faster as the planet pulled her earthward. The female peregrine falcon flaunted her status as the fastest animal who has ever lived on this earth.

On the other side of the same planet, another female aviator had, earlier in the day, taken flight as well but for entirely different reasons.

CHAPTER 2
THE EMPTY QUARTER, SAUDI ARABIA

The aircraft, recently put back together by the ground crew, flew straight and honest, cleaving the hot desert air, bumping occasionally in heat-driven thermal updrafts. Its single engine spit out a blast of rolling thunder echoing off the sand passing rapidly beneath the jet's belly. In the cramped cockpit, the airplane's sole occupant was not disturbed by the howling power plant under her fingertip control. She could barely hear it. Isolated and insulated against the mayhem outside; while traveling at 420 knots, (480 mph), the loudest noise she heard was her own breathing inside her oxygen mask. Most of the ear-splitting sound was left far behind and rather quickly. The noise that did penetrate the cockpit was inaudible. The liquid-filled earphones in her padded helmet were that good.

The F-16's cockpit served as her refuge. Not only did it keep out extraneous noise, it fended off troubles and problems generated on the ground, back at her base. Normally, but not always.

After major maintenance, regulations require a fighter plane to be flown by the squadron test pilot to check out whether all systems are operating correctly and to determine whether the aircraft is safe to fly. After the repairs are evaluated, and if the craft passes, a test hop offers the pilot a great opportunity to have fun with a supersonic jet. With the assigned portion of the mission, the evaluation flight, complete, a pilot has unbounded freedom to do as she wants. Until the fuel runs low, that is.

Normally this particular fighter jock would use free time in the F-16 to practice advanced air combat maneuvers, honing her skills, and trying new techniques. But not today, and not now.

Freedom of the skies usually offered an escape, a respite, a few minutes of highly focused effort and personal self-evaluation. *How did that max-rate turn go? Did I hold my head up under six Gs?"* she often asked herself during similar informal training. She prided herself in being able to endure high G loading and still function, still think, and still act, when her body weight was multiplied by six. Even if six times 120 pounds is not that terrific a task to bear.

Today had dawned differently and the test flight was not proceeding normally. She lacked the motivation to hone her deadly set of unique aviation skills. A recent conversation with her squadron commander, an older man, preyed on her mind, diverting her attention. He presented an opportunity to her. No, not an opportunity, as he pitched it. He expressed more of a demand for personal payment in return for future services rendered.

The way forward did not appear apparent to her. She needed to make a vital decision back on the ground and soon.

Perhaps a more demanding flight profile might cleanse her head. Saudi Arabia's Empty Quarter reminded the pilot of her home in West Texas. Dirty blue skies, flat terrain, a sandy expanse, and desolation stretched away on all sides. Only here, unlike her native Texas, the desert appeared to be much drier, sandier, and there were no signs of civilization. No dry farms, no cotton fields, no oil wells, no hardscrabble towns met her view in any direction. The wasteland beneath her was the reason the U. S. Air Force designated this area for test flights. The jet thunder affected no one but a few wandering Bedouins and their flea-bitten camels. If things went drastically wrong during the flight, the aircraft's impact with the ground would scarcely be noticed in the Empty Quarter.

At medium altitude, the dusty desert sky offered a metaphor of the choices before her back at base. A climb to higher, cleaner, more rarefied air was readily available by raising the aircraft's nose. Or she could level turn left or bank right and divert her flight path into new, uncharted territory. The fourth choice could be to descend, to go down. Those alternatives still left her time to think, to worry, to plan, and while analogous to her impending decision, settled nothing. A reboot of her mind lay below her, far below. A descent into another realm of flight offered its appeal. Getting "into the weeds," as the pilot community called it, suggested to her the best course of action would be to get down and dirty, not thinking about anything else.

She pointed the F-16's nose below the horizon and descended to 500 feet above the burning sand. This low altitude required increased attention to her pilotage but was still comfortable. The overlying mental problem returned in her mind's eye, "What to do?" A further descent to 250 feet, as shown on the radar altimeter, increased her workload. A moments' inattention, a hiccup, a twitch, and she would fly out of the sky and into the world. Now at very low level, the desert on either side of the F-16 was visible only laterally in vivid detail starting a quarter mile off each wingtip. Closer in, the world became a featureless, reddish stream passing by.

Exhilarating, but not yet good enough. She let down gradually to 100 feet above the wind-sculpted dunes. Finally, 100 percent of her focus had to be on operating the jet. The solid world comes at you rapidly at 100 feet and 480 mph. The slightest mistake would throw a greasy smear of fire and smoke across the ground as her life and the aircraft would disappear together in an instant fireball.

At this speed and this altitude, the only things she could visually recognize were directly in front of the windscreen, seconds out. Everything else in sight was a russet streak, a frantic blur. Everything else left her mind. Her internal problems were erased by the need for speed. Her coming decision was temporarily left behind with the jet's exhaust. The female pilot kept the little jet down on the sand, enjoying the required focus and forgetting all else until the low fuel warning light illuminated.

Play time over, Melissa A. Taylor, call sign "Mousse," Captain, United States Air Force, started a climb, turning toward her base and the decision waiting there for her. What was she willing to give for something she really wanted?

CHAPTER 3
MORRO BAY CALIFORNIA

The falcon accelerated downward in her dive, as if mother earth reclaimed her own with gravity. As if the world disciplined a creature with the unbridled ambition to fly and the primal urge to escape from the grasping planet's surface. Wings tucked in, wedge-shaped tail streamlined, head and beak pointed into the slipstream, the bird plunged. She exceeded 100 mph, making only the smallest corrections in her flight path with imperceptible movements of her wing and tail feathers. At that speed, any over-correction would cause a tumble or spin with the aerodynamic forces tearing the peregrine apart.

Her gaze locked on to her desired prey, she aimed for the spot in space the dove headed to, not where it appeared to be at present. Conventional wisdom holds, erroneously, that brute animals have no sense of time. Yet, she was able to predict the location of her target by projecting its flight path into the future. As she approached the fast-moving intercept point, she adjusted her own vector. She steepened her dive even more to aim behind the struggling dove. Then she pulled out of her earthward-bound trajectory. The falcon extended her long legs with their massive talons out into the airstream howling past her, instantly increasing her aerodynamic drag. She reduced her airspeed with her legs, like using the speed brakes on a fighter plane. Her wings unfolded slightly, assuming a planform resembling the letter "M" seen from above. Close to the flock of doves at low altitude, she leveled off. The sharp vertical pullout and the still-fierce airspeed imposed a virtual load of over six Gs. For a second, the two-and-a-half-pound peregrine effectively weighed 15 pounds. Partially folded, her wings could easily stand the strain. They generated the G loading.

With 30 mph of overtake on the dove and when a few feet behind it, the falcon, wings fully extended now, reached forward with her talons. She grasped her prey with a snap. In another intercept scenario, the bird might have struck the dove with both feet balled into fists, knocking it unconscious, then circled around, diving to catch the falling bird. Not today, not with a gaggle of crows waiting nearby to steal a hard-earned meal. Her black claws locked over-center. No need to clinch a grip. The claws pierced the hapless dove in several places. Continuing to slow, she reached below her and severed the dove's spinal cord just behind its head, using a notch on her beak designed for that very purpose. Darkness took the dove instantly.

Laboring, carrying the dead ring-necked dove's extra weight, she fanned the air with her wings, climbing and avoiding the circling, cawing crows, and ignoring the screaming gulls. Birds of both species were glad the peregrine's victim was not among their flocks. Eventually she reached her aerie on Morro Rock's southern face and dropped the day's breakfast onto the sandy ledge. She landed, touching the earth lightly in the shade of a blunt overhang, and folded her weary wings. Time to rest and to dine.

After a few minutes, her mate also returned to their rocky home, carrying a fresh-caught shorebird. As is always the case with falcons, hawks, eagles, owls, and other birds of prey, the male measured one-third smaller than the female peregrine. He hunted slighter fare. After a few squawks of welcome, both birds tore into their respective kills with hooked beaks, holding the carcasses in place by standing on them. They exchanged fresh, red flesh morsels with each other. To share raw meat is a sign of fidelity and mutual affection in the no-nonsense, hard-edged domain of raptors.

Satiated, the two falcons settled down to experience the day, both motionless on the ledge overlooking the harbor entrance. The daily life of any apex predator is one of 23 hours of relaxed indolence plus one hour devoted to bloody savagery. Later in the afternoon, she would take off again to hunt after finding a single enjoyable meal to be not enough. Maybe she would just want to fly. Why? To enjoy the freedom of the sky, perhaps to patrol and police her territory. Peregrines are protective of their local domain, warding off other interloping birds of their kind. She also needed to keep an eye out for the crows. In the air, a single crow is no match for a peregrine but a murder, the collective noun for crows is "murder," can and will kill a hawk or owl. One can never be too careful concerning crows.

However, she might take wing only to be airborne. Flying purg es the minds of birds and humans alike, ridding them of extraneous thoughts, relaxing stress and cares, except when it doesn't. Far away, stress took precedence in an interaction between hunter and hunted. The prey in this aerial engagement was not a crippled dove but a frightened human being.

CHAPTER 4
KING KHALID AIR BASE, SAUDI ARABIA

Captain Marcel "Frenchie" Thibodeau of Lafayette, Louisiana, and the United States Air Force, in that order, released the wheel brakes holding his aircraft stationary. He stroked the single throttle smoothly forward into the full power position. A familiar push on his back, centered between his shoulder blades, told him the jet engine reported for duty. The plane accelerated relentlessly along the seemingly endless runway, the bit in its metaphorical teeth. Ahead, the asphalt appeared to merge seamlessly into space, shimmering into the featureless desert out on the far horizon. He would be airborne long before running out of hard surface.

His diminutive mount, an F-16 fighter jet, nicknamed by US Air Force officialdom as the "Fighting Falcon," did not represent the current state-of-the art. It was non-stealthy and thus visible and vulnerable to hostile radars and missiles. The little jet, though old, still possessed a sufficiently charismatic aura to excite, excess engine thrust to spare, and enough maneuverability to continually thrill its pilots. Aviators who flew the Fighting Falcon were proud of the F-16 and even prouder to be allowed to fly it. But military hardware effectiveness is independent of human emotion, however heartfelt and sincere.

F-16s were confined to combat flights only over the Persian Gulf and were strictly forbidden to venture into the far more dangerous Iranian airspace. There, sudden death awaited the unwary and the un-stealthy.

Flying speed effortlessly achieved, Frenchie raised the jet's needle nose a scant few degrees and the howling engine pushed the fighter forward into the scorching desert air. Wing flaps and undercarriage retracted quickly, cleaning up the airframe, and reducing drag resulting in even faster acceleration. Under friendly radar control, he began a slight left bank and a steep climb toward the Strait of Hormuz, his patrol area for the day's mission. At last shed of the ground and departing the arid wasteland of Saudi Arabia, he exhaled a sigh of relief into his oxygen mask. He and the jet soon left the earth's dusty domain and entered the relatively clean and unspoiled realm of the sky. It is a free world unknown to terra-bound humans but familiar and comfortable to both pilots and soaring birds. He hoped to leave behind in the engine's turbulent exhaust the cares and concerns of service in the Air Force. Perhaps to abandon the everyday problems of life itself and the aching boredom of existence "downrange" as the squadron's pilots referred to their temporary residence in the Middle East.

Frenchie usually felt at home in the air, mentally focused and in full control of his immediate fate. For two or three hours, he would be on his own, alone with his airplane, his mission, and his thoughts. Only the ground radar controller's disembodied voice over the radio would keep him company. Terrestrial considerations tended to be discarded behind with altitude gained, fading into blurry insignificance as he climbed into the heavens, or what passed for heaven, over the barren desert. The desolate land below seemed to embody the concept of "God-forsaken."

The brown layer below thankfully blanketed the parched ground, hiding the sweeping sands fought over for centuries in never-ending religious wars. Such historical conflicts appeared picayune and petty when seen from extreme altitude. The Middle East desert appeared God-forsaken from above, but was anything but that on the surface. Contending armed sects continually clashed, each proudly claiming to be doing God's will. Far from being God forsaken, the wasteland over which Frenchie flew had for millennia seen entirely too much of what local religious fanatics knew as the true God, the one who they alone worshiped.

Frenchie lived for the freedom of the air, enjoying the mental concentration required to pilot a supersonic fighter jet regardless of how obsolete that jet was judged to be by Pentagon grandees. He knew the freedom of the skies by the term "Slipping the surly bonds of Earth" from a poem familiar to generations of pilots both civilian and military.

Many years prior, Pilot Officer John Gillespie Magee Jr., an American serving with the Royal Canadian Air Force, earned his reputation as an expert fighter pilot and a better poet. He wrote about "Slipping the surly bonds" in a poem, *High Flight*, chronicling the joys of solitary flight and the clean and pure and simple and beautiful life waiting just above the clouds.

Gillespie died in an airplane crash, in a mid-air collision with a squadron mate. His death illustrated how peace and terror often live in the same patch of sky, a fact Frenchie acknowledged deep inside himself but one he tried not to consider for too long.

This mission, like so many others, was predicted to be uneventful--boring holes in the sky and flying repetitive racetrack-shaped orbits at altitude. Still, flight was flight. The aviation process promised to purge his soul and clear his mind, if only for a few precious hours.

Welcome airborne peace came to Frenchie under the trappings of war. His jet carried the latest air-to-air missiles, nicknamed "Peregrine" by the bureaucratic powers that be. His aircraft's gun contained high-explosive cannon rounds. A combat sortie, make no mistake. It said so right on the squadron's posted flying schedule. The irony of achieving some mental respite through patrolling the lethal sky while armed to kill did not escape Frenchie. He gave the subject not much thought either. Nearly always, these flights turned out to be uneventful airplane rides. But it was an excellent day for an airplane ride. It was also a superb day to be a fighter pilot. What day or night is not? He did not, could not, know this flight would begin a series of actions, the results changing his life forever.

At his patrol altitude, he checked in with radar control and cruised, alone at last with the airplane doing all the routine work. The F-16 Fighting Falcon was aerodynamically unstable. Even straight-and-level flight required constant, almost instantaneous adjustments by the flight control computer or else the aircraft would pitch up vertically. The resulting aerodynamic stresses would break the aircraft into sizeable pieces. Vital actions taken by the computer were undetectable by its pilot, but were there all the same as various control surfaces flexed, bending the surrounding airflow.

Above him, the sky radiated with an indigo intensity never seen on the earth's surface. Darker directly overhead, the dark blue color of truth, the heavens faded to gray-blue ambiguity around the 360-degree horizon. Far below, he could barely make out through the dusty haze the shorelines of the countries bordering the Strait of Hormuz; Saudi Arabia to the south, the Emirates to the southwest, and hostile Iran to the north. Even these lines of geographical and political demarcation dissolved into blurry nothingness toward the distant hazy boundary of sky and earth. Without GPS input and the radar controller's supervision, he could easily become lost and off course.

With no clouds to gage his speed by and no landmarks visibly passing below, Frenchie felt suspended motionless in mid-air. He was detached from the corrupted Earth yet not of the pure, dark heavens above. He existed frozen in a blinding-bright version of the "twilight zone." This is the domain is experienced by open-ocean scuba divers who can see neither the surface above nor the sea floor below. No sensation of velocity, only his instruments told him he traveled at a large percentage of the speed of sound. Despite the torrent of air rushing by the cockpit and the thundering engine behind him, little noise reached his ears inside his sound-isolated helmet. The din could not penetrate his foam-filled earphones. He flew alone with his thoughts, but not fast enough to escape them.

Usually, the isolation of high altitude calmed him, a relief from quotidian surface worries and cares. But sadly, not today. For the umpteenth time, he wondered, *"What the hell was going on back in Phoenix."* Communication with Yvette by email had always been unsatisfying, impersonal, and remote. Lately, things became worse with cryptic notes written in a hurry. Typos and misspelled words marred the few short sentences of each brief message. The scant actual contact with his wife hurt. He missed her laughing smile, her long, raven hair, and her Louisiana accent echoing his own drawl. Most of all, he missed her lithe body, nude beside him, alluring, receptive, bordering on wanton.

Images came flooding back to his mind's eye. Jackson Square, New Orleans; strolling the historic French Quarter in the quiet cool of the morning. They returned to their second-floor hotel room with its wrought-iron balcony to make love in the humid heat of the afternoon, floor-to-ceiling windows wide open to the street noises below.

Where had those days gone? The wheels of time spun like the ceiling fan's slow rotation above the wet, tangled sheets. How did it all get so disconnected? He knew his repeated deployments and lengthy absences were a strain on her. Daily flights offered him a break. She enjoyed no similar outlet, only the workaday existence of everyday life as a married woman with the other half of her partnership on the other side of the planet.

Yet, he asked himself, did he miss his spouse for her companionship or merely the sex she used to share willingly, enjoying each other mightily and nightly? For whatever reason, he still ached for Yvette.

A radio call blew away his introspective thoughts. In his earphones, the voice seeming to emanate from the center of his skull.

"Falcon One, vector three zero zero. Confirmed bandit at two zero miles. Weapons hot," the female controller said.

"Holy shit! A hot vector! An enemy target 20 miles to the northwest!" Gone instantly was the romantic revelry in his head, replaced by the urgent mission at hand.

Responding instinctively to years of intensive training, Frenchie entered the "zone." Experienced primarily by predatorial raptors and combat fighter pilots, the zone is a mental place. Time slows to a crawl and thought processes kick into hyper-drive. It is a domain where laser focus is normal and fear has no leverage. Failure is not a conscious option and the risk of sudden death is not allowed to degrade or to interfere with ongoing vital tasks.

His hands flitted around the cramped cockpit preparing for airborne battle. He jammed the throttle into full power, armed the short-range missiles using the weapons computer, then returned to the stick and throttle to activate the aircraft's radar. The radar gave him extended, multi-mile vision, reaching out, looking for the aircraft identified as a "bandit," an enemy. He quickly found the target displayed on the radar scope and locked onto it. Following its pilot's commands, the little jet accelerated through Mach One, the speed of sound. Frenchie flew toward where the target was headed, not where it appeared to be at present. The bandit, until now a hypothetical entity, represented a live human being in mortal danger.

Disoriented and frightened, the Iranian pilot was hopelessly lost. Flying an obsolete Russian aircraft, a

MiG-29, he was in serious trouble. Mullahs chose the young Persian for Islamic Iranian Air Force pilot training due in part to his religious fervor. His bushy black beard interfered with his oxygen mask's seal against his face. Life-giving gas leaked away unbreathed. Without it, mental processes slowed down, confusion reigned, and decision-making became difficult. Oxygen deficiency-generated confusion had caused him to mishandle his radio controls. No one talked to him. No one could tell him about the F-16 rapidly approaching on a collision course, silently stalking him at supersonic speed, traveling faster than the shock waves generated behind it.

With his radar locked on, Frenchie closed the distance between the two aircraft rapidly. What had been invisible seconds before became a tiny dot just above the horizon. Before his eyes, the speck grew and took on the outline of an airplane. Time for the U. S. Air Force pilot to decide whether to kill or not. The American radar controller made the easy choice for him.

"Falcon One cleared to fire," she said.

The controller's voice, normally the epitome of studied cool detachment, betrayed her emotions with a noticeable rise in pitch and the hurried urgency of command.

The voice in the center of his skull told Frenchie exactly what he wanted to hear. Obeying the controller as well as his own aggressiveness, he pulled the trigger on the control stick at the word "Cleared...."

A pencil-thin Peregrine missile left the wing in a rush, leaving a smoke trail behind its rocket motor, a wispy white path leading forward to death in the sky. The missile possessed a focused mind and a single eye of its own. It locked its seeker, peering through a Cyclops glass dome, on the distant target. Instead of homing directly in on the enemy plane, the Peregrine's computer predicted where the Iranian would be soon. It steered the missile to the future intercept point. The Peregrine hit the Iranian fighter just behind the cockpit, detonating the missile's explosive warhead, instantly igniting a burning fuel fireball. The hapless pilot perceived a bone-crushing impact and an instantaneous flash of intense pain, then the darkness mercifully took him.

Frenchie followed the missile's flight path until the Iranian aircraft exploded. Maneuvering violently, he barely missed the tumbling fireball. As the F-16 turned tightly, the G forces built rapidly because of the narrow turn radius of the F-16 and its blazing airspeed. Six Gs registered on the cockpit gage and Frenchie's 180 pounds of weight became effectively over 1000 pounds. He did not notice nor care. He turned the jet toward home base and, with the radar controller's permission, began a descent to the world on the ground.

Back at the air base, Frenchie turned into the traffic pattern, flying down the runway at 1500 feet altitude. Midway, he pulled the F-16's nose a few degrees above the horizon and rolled the aircraft. In two seconds, the sky was replaced by the earth and then it re-established itself over the cockpit canopy. The classic victory roll owes its origin to World War II. It is thoroughly prohibited by the flight safety organization of the United States Air Force. Not one to boast, during his letdown to the airfield, he debated internally about performing a prohibited vulgar display of bravado. However, some traditions must be followed, dictated by generations of fighter pilots. Frenchie banked the Fighting Falcon to land to a waiting celebration of his unexpected, unplanned aerial triumph.

CHAPTER 5
KING KHALID AIR BASE, SAUDI ARABIA

The congratulatory celebrations petered out, his back aching from slapping. His gloved right hand was shaken nearly off while his helmet bag was carried off the flight line by squadron mates. But all this hoopla ended. To his complete surprise, Frenchie achieved any fighter pilot's supreme goal, a mid-air destruction of another fighter plane in single-warrior combat.

Air-to-air engagements are rare in today's world of warfare, particularly when American pilots are up against second or third world countries. Flying the F-16, no longer the premier air superiority fighter plane, made Frenchie's triumph even more unlikely.

His friends had waited to welcome him upon landing. Their well-wishes seemed sincere, if tinged green with envy. The sweltering crowd on the parking ramp, baking under the desert sun, dispersed seeking shade. He thanked his ground crew for providing him with a reliable aircraft and with deadly missiles. They would paint an Iranian flag on the fuselage below the cockpit, signifying a victory for that plane. Across the empty tarmac, he headed off alone, just as he had flown the mission, solo, to the wing headquarters. Debriefing the action with the air intelligence troops was his last mission requirement. They would glean significant information about Iranian air operations from his personal account of the day's air combat.

In the rabbit's warren of pre-fab buildings serving as the head shed, his squadron commander stopped him. He was a man whose presence at the impromptu meetings beside the cooling F-16 rang significantly by his absence. Normally, the commander and designated leader of a fighter squadron would be the first to shake a victorious pilot's hand as the returning aviator dismounted his plane. But not this time. The lieutenant colonel was nowhere to be seen. He was not missed by the attendees.

The commander, Lieutenant Colonel Ralph, "Bull" Conner measured five foot nine, three inches shorter than Frenchie. He was built like a fireplug. Short-cropped graying hair adorned a round head set on a thick neck and a stocky body. Bull's face featured a lantern jaw he thrust out when making a point, particularly to a lowly subordinate. If he was bothered by being assigned a call sign, a nickname, inspired by an infamous segregationist sheriff, he hid it well.

"Thibodeau, boy, I've been looking for you," the commander growled. His strident voice echoed along the narrow corridor; his accent unmistakable.

Trapped in the empty on passageway, Frenchie put his back up against the wall, stood at attention, and looked straight ahead, over Conner. The contrast could not have been greater, the trim, soft-spoken Cajun confronted by the loud, pugnacious officer from East Texas.

"Captain, I'm disappointed in you. Where have you been?" the commander spoke first, his voice a decibel too intense.

"Sir? I just came in from the ramp," Frenchie replied.

"You did a victory roll over the runway today. You know that's against regulations, don't you?" Bull's jaw shoved forward, closer to Frenchie's face.

"Yes sir, I did it and I understand it's not recommended. I got carried away."

"If you hadn't bagged that scumbag Iranian, I would have grounded you. I mean rules to be followed. Have I made myself clear?"

"Yes sir, message received loud and clear," Frenchie said with only a hint of irony. A half-smile played across his face.

Conner studied Frenchie's face, looking up at him. With a grimace, the squadron commander pivoted on his heel and stomped off along the hallway without another word. His booted footsteps rang louder than any speech he might have made.

Frenchie exhaled a sigh of relief and continued toward the intelligence shop. He did not see any need to point out to his annoyed immediate superior if he had not shot down the MiG-29, he would not have performed the victory roll. Conner's antagonism against him had been obvious since Frenchie first signed into the squadron on deployment. The underlying reason for the overt hostility remained a mystery to the bemused captain.

Later that evening, at the all-ranks dining facility, aka the "chow hall," Frenchie picked up a battered plastic tray and entered the cafeteria-style queue. A grizzled chief master sergeant, his exalted rank usually verbally shortened to "Chief," held court behind a table at beginning of the parade of diners. He welcomed his hungry charges and engaged each one in brief conversation. The senior enlisted person in the squadron, Chief Bichet took his supervisory responsibilities seriously. The older man, a burly Creole from New Orleans, knew Frenchie well, even across the rank, racial, and generational divides. Louisiana has that effect on people who call the swampland home.

Empty tray in hand, the captain surveyed the steam table and its selection of food the US Air Force provided for its troops on deployment.

"*Bon Soir*, what's less bad today chief? *Jambalaya? Filé gumbo?* Crayfish e*toufée?*" Frenchie grinned, expecting the usual joshing *repartée* between the two "Coon Asses" as natives of Louisiana tend to call themselves. He expected familiar camaraderie, a few words of Cajun/Creole French, and a welcome bit of normality ending a day which had been anything but normal.

The older man leaped to his feet, snapped to rapt attention, and rendered a crisp hand salute to the captain, an official military courtesy not required indoors but one extended in exceptional circumstances as a sign of respect.

"Congratulations on the shoot-down, captain," the old sergeant replied, his voice deep into the bass register, his creole accent flowing like honey on the rock. "My expert cooks tell me they have a stash of off-menu steaks squirreled away in the cooler. Would you go for one to celebrate?"

"*Merci beaucoup*, chief, that sounds *trés bien. Laissez les bons temps roulez!*"

"How do you want it cooked and what do you want to drink with it?"

"Very rare, *s'il vous plaît*, cold and blue in the middle. I'd really like three fingers of Tennessee sippin' whisky, but I'd better have sweet iced tea instead, like down home in our bayou country."

Saudi Arabia's puritanical ruling clerics were happy to welcome American military personnel in-country to defend the kingdom, to protect the widely extended royal family, and to keep gross infidels from defiling the two holy places of Islam. As long as those intrepid aerial warriors didn't pour themselves a drink of Koran-banned demon rum while doing so. The primitive mullahs forbad any alcohol on the air base, a hardship not willingly endured by many hard-drinking fighter pilots.

Worse yet, female service members were compelled to cover up in burka-like garments when off base and to wear head coverings beyond standard military hats and ball caps. Evidently, the sight of a few square inches of bare female American skin or a loose lock of blonde hair might drive devout Saudi men into uncontrollable spasms of desire. Consequently, few Americans ventured off base and fewer women went "outside the wire."

By and by, a profusely sweating cook flopped a huge steak, lightly browned and seared with cross-hatched grill marks, on Frenchie's tray. The hunk of meat, still sizzling, lapped over the paper plate's edges and exuded a rich grilled beef aroma. A generous scoop of instant mashed potatoes with white gravy and a ladled torrent of green peas soon joined it. The sergeant carefully placed a plastic glass half-filled with a light brown liquid next to the groaning tray, along with an enormous bottle of Tabasco sauce.

"Good work today sir, they'll hear about this *trés bienôt* on Bayou Teche," the older man promised.

In celebrating Frenchie's combat victory, the chief recognized peak performance under pressure. He dealt with pressure every day. His dining customers, military personnel all, showed up on time expecting their meals to be hot and ready. They were also highly food-opinionated and often heavily armed. Accordingly, the Chief ran a tight ship in the chow hall.

Diners in the chow hall self-segregated themselves in seating. Groups clustered at long tables by rank, unit affiliation, professional specialty, or gender, but never by race. Frenchie's squadron mates expected him to join them and to relive the day's aerial combat in colorful language with much waving of his hands in simulated flight. His account also needed to be punctuated by subtle boasting and faux humility.

"Hey fighter ace! Come, tell us how you did it," one pilot called out across the noisy room.

In return, Frenchie merely shook his head "No" and continued alone to an empty table. The details and the tone of the debriefing in the intelligence shop had caused him to consider what he had done. His aerial victory involved the killing of another human being. His was not a victory over a peer, over another proficient pilot who knew the risks, who had accepted a challenge to an aerial dual. The engagement was not air combat as much as it was the airborne murder of an obviously lost and low-skilled Iranian. The ground radar troops had tracked the MiG-29's flight path and the intelligence monitors had heard the Iranian ground controllers frantically trying to make radio contact. He knew that now. The knowledge had taken all the joy out of the offered celebration.

Eschewing any of the clustered groups, Frenchie sat down by himself. The serious look on his face told anyone watching he was not up for reliving the day's combat and for his squadron mates to cut him some serious slack. Slicing a bite from the enormous, borderline raw steak, he dug in, knowing the top sergeant watched from behind his desk. He raised the plastic glass to drink. Instead of the wimpy perfume of weak, sweet iced tea, the sharp esters of Tennessee sour mash whisky tempered by sweetness infused by charred oak barrels assaulted his nostrils. The libation represented Lynchburg, Tennessee's best, served straight up. There was no mistaking the flavor. After a second tongue-searing sip, a slight shadow fell over the table. Frenchie looked up to see a familiar, but not nearly familiar enough, female figure standing across from him.

The youthful woman pulled out a plastic stacking chair and asked, "Mind if I join you? You look like you need a little company."

Her voice needed to be just a bit louder than normal conversational level to cut through the verbal din echoing through the chow hall. Even with the background noise, her words rang distinctly, re-enforced by some inferred certainty and authority. She sat down, placing her own tray across from his without waiting for an answer.

The joining captain stood five foot seven, slender with short blonde hair and dancing blue eyes. Her baggy flight suit's name tag read "Taylor." It sported the same squadron patches attached with Velcro and the same fearsome logos as Frenchie's own sweaty "goat skin."

Melissa Taylor's reputation in the unit was one of relentless good humor. However, those laughing eyes turned steel blue and flint hard when briefing or debriefing a mission. To discuss a flight, she flashed a look signifying stone-cold seriousness with fire in her eyes. Melissa also flaunted serious cred as one of the most proficient F-16 pilots in the wing. Her exalted status stemmed from her ability to dog fight at close range, the designed domain of aerial superiority for the Fighting Falcon. In a twisting, turning, stomach-churning fur ball, few pilots, male or female, could best Melissa Taylor once she visually locked-on to her hapless opponent.

Pilots' call signs, their distinctive individual nicknames, get assigned informally by their squadron mates. A matter of considerable thought, an individual's call sign may be based on some outstanding physical attribute. A stocky pilot would be "Slim" a slim one might be "Splinter" A bald guy could be "Curly." Alternately, a nickname could be a play on the squadron member's family name. The family name "Roach" will always be preceded by "Bug." A "Rhodes" has to be "Dusty." Marcel Thibodeau could only be "Frenchie" or maybe "Gator." Due to his dark Gallic looks, narrow build, and hawk's nose, "Frenchie" it had to be. The individual concerned has no say in the selection of his or her call sign. Attempting to choose one's own call sign is considered bad form in the U. S. Air Force. Chief Bichet would call such an attempt *trés gauche*.

Because of her thinness, cheery grin, and diminutive stature, Melissa Taylor's call sign became "Moose." In jest, she feminized the nickname by spelling it "Mousse" after a hair care product she never appeared to use.

After she scooted her chair closer to the table and slowly crossed her legs, Frenchie looked intently across at her and replied, "Sure, have a seat, Mousse."

She stared at the rare steak on his plate; one notch missing, its purple interior oozing beef *jus* and blood, the smell of seared beef rising in the air.

"I've seen cows hurt worse than that and get over it."

Her West Texas accent oozed like prickly pear syrup.

Frenchie laughed and asked, "Would you like half? No way I can finish this and the chief won't give me any dessert unless I do."

"Sure, as long as you haven't drenched it with Tabasco sauce."

He reached over the table, picked up her knife and fork, sliced off a generous portion of meat and placed it gently on her plate, which looked to be occupied solely by green salad. As they consumed the steak in silence together, she wrinkled her pert nose, reached for his paper cup without asking permission, sniffed the contents once, twice, and took a hearty swig.

"You must have some serious pull with the chief from NOLA."

"I do, but who knows why? Maybe it's Cajun-Creole *rapprochement* or swamp solidarity."

Conversation lagged awkwardly as they ate. Usually vivacious and talkative, Mousse remained strangely quiet, her eyes often looking off into the unseen middle distance. Frenchie focused on his own thoughts. Finally, she pursed her full lips and spoke.

"You're not whooping it up with the guys and gals. Why? They'll want a full debrief. It's not every day one of us scores a MiG kill."

"The engagement was a piece of cake. More like an execution than actual air combat," Frenchie replied.

"It's not a straightforward thing to do, killing another human being, no matter what the rules of engagement say. Not that I'd know, never having ever been on a hot vector," Mousse said.

"You're right. It's easier said than done."

She took a long look at his expression and dropped the subject like a 500-pound bomb. By the time he finished his portion of the steak, fixings, and the half-glass of Jack Daniel's he felt well-satiated and he experienced the alcohol's buzzy effects. With booze and with sex, a few months of forced absence heightens both the desire for, and the pleasures of, catching up on lost opportunities. He checked one square with the Tennessee whiskey, but not the other. His brain raced, searching for a way to broach the sensitive second objective with his comely dining companion.

"The boss had it in for you today with his threat of grounding." Mousse broke the awkward silence with a verbal change of direction.

"How do you know about that?"

"I was in the intel shop. Conner's voice carries."

"Ah, the walls have ears. Think I'll step outside," he said. "This isn't the place for that conversation."

It also was not the place for the other conversation he intended to start. The side entrance to the mess hall led to a short landing with a rough-cut board railing. After sunset, the desert cools off rapidly. The bracing night air tried in vain to un-fog his brain. He leaned on the handrail and drank in the dry oxygen. In the distance, shimmering in the day's residual heat re-radiated by acres of tarmac, he saw see the multitude of lights marking the airfield. The desert's silence was ripped from time to time with the howling of jet engines as aircraft took to the star-studded sky. He heard the door behind him open and close. He sensed her feminine presence nearby. No need to turn around to see who re-joined him.

"You're not the only one with problems in coping with Bull Conner," she said. "I've had my run-ins with him too."

Frenchie slowly turned to face her. The desert breeze blew her flight suit against her draped figure, her soft curves visible even in the near-dark. Her blonde hair fell across her face and she flicked the locks back with one hand, the hand wearing the obligatory, complex, fighter pilot wrist watch.

"What's your problem with our fearless leader?" He got right to the point.

Before her answer, the distant thunder of a take-off from the airfield interrupted their exchange. She spent the brief interval during which normal communication would be difficult looking past Frenchie toward the invisible black horizon.

"Not now, this isn't the time nor the place to get into that," she said, reversing the subject tables on Frenchie. Her tone of voice told him to not pursue the unstated issue.

Changing the subject once again, she went off on a different, more windward tack. "Do you think about the guy you killed today?"

"Yeah, I will, someday, but I'll try not to until then. He would have gleefully done the same to me if he could've hacked the mission. But tonight, I didn't feel like celebrating the killing of another guy, another pilot. That's why I sat down to eat by myself."

"And that's why I joined you. Hope you don't mind. So, as a martyr in a holy war he's now been issued 72 virgins and you, the local hero, almost got grounded."

Frenchie looked the earnest woman straight in the eye for a long few seconds. She returned the attention, their gazes locked-on to each other. He deduced this was his best chance at seduction.

"Speaking of virgins---." He did not get to finish his suggestive thought.

"Don't even think about it. You're not my type, or at least I don't believe so. Besides, I can't pass the physical," she replied at last, looking away from Frenchie out toward the airfield.

"I can't not think about it. I can be your type. I can take your breath away, Mousse."

"No. You couldn't, we shouldn't. You're married. That's why you're probably not my type."

She ended the exchange and turned to go without speaking. However, including the word "probably" gave him a reason to hope for the future. Frenchie watched her enter the chow hall, silhouetted against the bright interior, the wind rippling her flight suit, outlining her slender hips and her high, rounded ass. He wondered if his direct, carnal approach had been too direct.

While his ship of seduction had run aground on the unforgiving rocks of traditional morality, he was not going to, would not, abandon the effort. The internal longing ached too strongly. He yearned for sexual release and/or for feminine companionship. What urge drove him most? Did the actual reason matter? Could Mousse be the temporary replacement for both, filling the void left by Yvette's emotional and geographical distance? He surprised himself with his clumsy come-on. It was not a planned maneuver but rather a spur-of-the-moment verbal lapse revealing a desire he had long recognized but one he tried to deny.

She instantly recognized his intent with his comment referring to virgins. Did it mean she entertained the similar thoughts? Or, was she used to comments like that from chauvinistic male squadron mates? Despite his dinning choice of solo seating, she did plunk her ass down in front of him. A day filled with aerial triumph which would normally bring deep satisfaction aided by a rare steak and three fingers of Jack Daniels was ending with too many unanswered questions. Unable to come up with answers he could endure contemplating for long, Frenchie opened the door to the chow hall. Mousse was nowhere in sight.

Sexual rituals do not always pay off for every participant. When these plans succeed, the result is magical in the world of humans and in the domain of raptors alike.

CHAPTER 6
MORRO BAY, CALIFORNIA

The longing grew for over a week, swelling stronger and more difficult to ignore with each passing day. The early onset of what passes for spring in mild, costal California, the rapid increase in daylight hours, triggered winter-dormant hormones in the female and male peregrines. Chemicals coursing in their blood, affecting their brains, urged them to mate. It was time to procreate, to perpetuate their species. Perhaps they could achieve a measure of inner satisfaction for having done so, along with the resulting carnal knowledge of each other.

She took to the air first, circling high over Morro Rock, enjoying the freedom of the sky, waiting for him. The multitudinous shore birds warily watched the orbiting falcon from below, unsure of her intentions. Did she look for sex or for prey?

He joined her, climbing directly from their aerie, and circled in synch with her. Both falcons traced clockwise orbits facing each other dozens of feet apart, 300 feet in the air. Their cries, high-pitched screeches, "Scree!

Scree!" each echoed by the other, carried down to the nervous food-flocks near the surface. The shorebirds relaxed and resumed the quotidian activities of their daily life, however short those lives were destined to be. They all knew and understood, with knowledge embedded in their inherited memory, that falcons hunt silently. The chirps and shrieks broadcast a sure signal the pair of predators were obsessed, were possessed, by mutually felt imperatives, not the stalking of prey, at least not yet.

The two birds' opposing circles tightened, their radii reduced, sexual attraction drew them together as if by an invisible magnetic force. Around and around they went, at a constant altitude and speed, their calls becoming more distinct and louder. After a few more orbits, the peregrines wheeled tighter, pulling Gs in their turns, their wingtips almost touching. Then, they relaxed their aerial quadrille and resumed traveling larger individual paths across the skies, counter-clockwise this time.

The male rolled out into level flight and climbed. His wings clawed for altitude until he reached a hundred feet above her. Folding his wings in the "M" configuration, head vertical, he simulated an intercept dive, called a "stoop," aiming toward the centers of her invisible circles in the air.

He pulled out with max Gs below her height and took up his orbit again. She replicated his maneuver with a playful mock stoop of her own and resumed pacing him. Stoop demonstrations validated the prospective mates' personal hunting and provisioning ability and their physical fitness to do just that.

There appeared no genuine need for these airborne courtship displays. Falcons mate for life. The two had been together as hunting partners and mates for four years. But natural conventions must always be obeyed. More than just an empty ritual, athletic participation in the aerial ballet stimulated the hormones running through their bodies and further drove the breeding imperatives they both experienced.

The male left the mid-air mating dance and flew south toward Morro harbor and its swampy sea estuary while she continued to wheel and soar in place near the rock. She remained silent now. Ten minutes later, he returned, his talons clutching a small, dead, brown bird, a fresh kill.

The female saw him coming from afar and turned to meet him. She dove below his altitude on an opposing, head-on course. Before reaching his shadow, she began a vertical climb and a half loop, ending up beneath him, inverted, her black and white variegated belly exposed to the sun. Her mate descended the scant three feet separating them and handed off the deceased bird in mid-air. Her talons locked onto the ritual food offering. She rolled back right side up and started a shallow glide toward their domicile on the rock, carrying the mating meal with her.

After a few more patrol orbits to sweep the general vicinity of any potential rivals, the male peregrine followed her home. He landed lightly beside her on the rocky ledge, folding his wings, which had just served him well.

After plucking and devouring parts of the fresh-caught breakfast, they consummated their relationship. The female bent over on her long legs, allowing him to mount her from the rear while he held her steady with his wings. They would continue the coupling process again and again most of the morning, then rest until it became time to hunt again, before dusk. As darkness fell, they would, unlike humans, become dormant, relaxed at night, and comforted by the benign blackness.

Mating dances are not confined to the world of birds, often playing out between prospective human partners as well.

Chapter 7
King Khalid Air Base, Saudi Arabia

The fluorescent shop light, the only illumination in the room, hovered low above the pool table, casting its white, antiseptic glow onto the dead-level expanse of green felt. Darkness dominated outside the table's brightly lit domain, growing denser with distance until the room's walls faded into invisibility. At three o'clock in the morning, all was silent except for the clicks of colliding *faux* ivory balls. The occasional distant roar of jet engines echoed from the runway far off in the desert night.

Two figures circled the table, lining up their shots, and taking great care to avoid each other while playing. Each became visible as they stepped up to play. Each in turn faded back into obscurity, moving away, holding onto their pool cues, and keeping the field of contest between them after a missed shot. One a male, the other a female, both in worn flight suits and dusty combat boots. Both were trying to come down from the addictive adrenaline rush generated by their just-completed night flights. Flying jet fighters is exciting. Flying those jets after dark is doubly so. The allowable margin of error shrinks, and the penalties for major mistakes are greater when hazards lurk unseen in the night. The two decompressed minus the alcohol traditionally used by aviators for facilitating recovery back to a ground-bound existence. Sleep would not return for either pilot until their systems purged themselves of the hormones coursing through their respective bloodstreams, hormones numbering more than one type.

Off-base recreational opportunities were nonexistent in Saudi Arabia, particularly those favored by young, virile military personnel. The chief desires for diversion of the denizens of the Air Force base were deemed "*haram*, sinful, and strictly forbidden by the primitive, overbearing Saudi religious police. These guardians of virtue and warriors against evil were easily identified by their calf-length white robes and the sticks they used to beat miscreants.

To compensate, the U. S. Air Force imported the equipment needed for letting off steam and for relaxation. These tended to be work-out gyms equipped with exercise machines and weights for lifting, plus the ever-popular video game parlor. But someone, probably a throwback or old head, brought in a high-quality, nine-foot competition pool table. He or she set it up in a dedicated room located off the chow hall. No batteries required for such analog entertainment; i.e. wielding pool cues and financially speculating on the outcome of matches. A few games around the table sometimes involved higher stakes when the players were alone late at night.

A white cue ball exploded the colored object balls from their tight triangle rack, sending them clattering around the table in the initial break. Frenchie paced, circled, cue in hand, looking for an achievable first move. His opponent orbited with him, always remaining on the opposite side of the playing field, out of reach.

"Two ball in the side pocket," he said, making the shot.

"Speaking of breaks, has Boss Conner busted your balls recently?" Mousse remarked unseen from the inky shadows.

"Are you trying to distract me?" Frenchie laughed, missing his second attempt at sinking a ball. "But the answer is no. I avoid him by night flying. Nobody over the rank of captain flies after dark. You know that."

He stepped back from the table into the shadows and Mousse replaced him in the cone of light. On the table's far side, she carefully lined up her shot.

"Mousse, is it time for you to dish the dirt on your own issues with our so-called leader?" he replied. "Inquiring minds want to know."

"Nine ball in the corner. I guess so. But this has to stay between you and me."

"No sweat, I know how to safeguard classified information," he said.

"I'm up for promotion to major soon and Conner writes my performance appraisal, the last one before the promotion board meets. Twelve ball in the side. He keeps inviting me alone to his quarters to "critique my performance."" Her voice wavered, tapering off into silence.

She missed the shot, an easy one, and backed off into the darkness, only not as far this time.

"Holy shit! So, that's it!" Frenchie said, then he asked an entirely unnecessary question.

"What performance does he want to evaluate? Have you gone to the OSI (Office of Special Investigations)? They're supposed to handle this sexual harassment crap. What are you going to do?" He too missed an easy shot, his cue wavering in mid-stroke.

Melissa moved closer to the lighted table and leaned on her vertical cue, studying the layout of the balls on the green field.

"No, the good colonel told me if I talked to anyone about this, it would be his word against mine; an experienced officer versus an emotional woman and me only a captain. I'd be labeled a troublemaker, not a team player. I don't know what I'll do. My ultimate goal, ever since I was a teenager in Texas, has been to command a fighter squadron, maybe move up to be a wing commander. I can't make it with a negative report card delaying me pinning on my major's leaves. Twelve ball in the side."

She waved her cue ineffectually at the shot and retreated into the darkness. He sank a ball, then another.

"So, you might go through with it. You'd prostitute yourself for a promotion?"

He instantly regretted using that exact phrasing. She did not react except to take a quick step further back. She slid sideways in the gloom as they circled the table, remaining opposite each other. Frenchie went on.

"Mousse, you are the hottest F-16 pilot I've ever flown with or against. Hotter in more ways than in fighter operations. You'd make an outstanding squadron leader. But, sweet Jesus, is that job worth the price he's demanding?" his voice rising in pitch, louder and strident.

He paused for a ten-count, going on. "If you go through with this, I'll support you and your first salute in your major's rank will come from me. Five ball in the corner."

She remained silent as he missed his next shot. She spoke up with a catch in her voice, stepping closer to the light. Even in the semi-darkness, he could see her eyes glistening and moist.

"I don't yet know what I'll do. But I do know your support means a lot to me. Most guys wouldn't care, wouldn't get involved. I'd never talk to them like I have with you."

She circled the table, halving the distance between them to stop in front of Frenchie for the first time during the match.

Mousse turned and bent far over to address the white ball, treating him to the sight of her thin flight suit pulled tight over her shapely ass. Her cue wobbled, she blew the shot, and she retreated a step, still illuminated by the pure white glow.

Turning to face him, she spoke across the three feet separating them. Her eyes flashed that fire he had only seen in flight briefings.

"Your move, captain."

Frenchie placed the first and second fingers of his left hand on the table's polished wooden bumper rail, leaving a narrow slit between them. His rigid cue slid easily into the tight gap and with a strong, straight surge, he sent the white ball the length of the table. It sank his object ball with a satisfying *twock* and backed slowly away from the pocket using reverse English.

Glancing back to her, he saw Mousse standing in the twilight with her cue held vertically between her legs, tip up. She wrapped the fingers of her left hand loosely around the cue six inches down from the end, her thumb on top of her coiled fingers. With her right hand, fingers curved, she stroked chalk on the padded tip.

"Thanks again Frenchie, for listening. I feel your support comes with respect. I've had feelings for you all along but I've tried to hide them. Desire, yes, but also a longing to get to know you. You're not like the other guys and it shows. Or at least to me it does."

Her eyes, even shaded by the overhead light, flashed. She walked to the door, locked it, and returned to face him, much nearer this time. He reached out with his left hand and bridged the scant distance between them. Never had he touched her except for the occasional high five. His fingertips caressed her cheek, starting just below her ear, trailing gently along her jaw to her chin. Moving closer, he raised her face to his and their lips met for the first time. Clattering, two pool cues fell to the floor when their arms enveloped each other. The kiss lasted for an eternity and was not long enough. Sliding his hands down her back and over her hips, he found her bottom to be as firm and round as he hoped and longed for.

She stepped back and in one long slow reveal, unzipped her flight suit. A shrug of her shoulders let the fireproof overall slide down to her boots. Black bikini panties followed, slipped off her hips with trembling fingers, whispering down her smooth legs. Her lacey bra found itself discarded.

Frenchie frantically fumbled with his own flight suit, the zipper stuck. When he solved the jam and looked up, Mousse had bent over the pool table, standing on the low stool used by short players to reach across the green expanse. He entered her from behind, finding the wet, slippery way easily, his hands grasping her tidy waist to clasp her tightly. Rarely had he been in such synch with a sexual partner. When both were exhausted, panting, and fulfilled, he fell out of her. Standing up from the table, she turned around and kissed him again, her arms around his neck, naked bodies pressed together.

She stepped back, pulled up her panties, and slowly zipped up her flight suit. Mousse looked intently into his eyes. She was silent now.

Taking her hands in his, he repeated his promise.

"Whatever you do, Whatever choice you make, I'm all in," he said, the double entendre did not go unnoticed by the smile on her face.

Turning to go, she spoke looking back over her shoulder.

"I've enjoyed about as much of this as I can stand. See you this evening, we brief at 1900."

She spun, disappearing into the dark. He heard the door open quickly, close slowly, and once again, he saw her silhouetted against the light from the chow hall. The glow haloed her blond hair and outlined her now-familiar body. They would meet again, this time on a mission.

CHAPTER 8
OVER SAUDI ARABIA

Mousse slowly, carefully slid her F-16 under the airborne tanker's tail with a slight increase in engine thrust. Flying close formation, she handled the little jet with infinite care, caressing the flight controls and the throttle with her gloved hands. Above her, the giant multi-engine tanker, a repurposed airliner, floated like a dark aluminum cloud in the night. It blocked her upward view to the unblinking stars, sheltering her like a mother hen. In the refueling position and in stable formation, she opened a tight receptacle on the fighter's spline, ready to receive a transfer of life-giving fuel from the flying gas station.

The boom operator extended the 30-foot rigid tube from the tanker's belly and thrust the nozzle into the waiting recess on the F-16. Hooked up, Mousse had little to do. She only had to maintain her position giving her time to think. The obvious sexual connotations of the air-to-air refueling act preyed on her mind as much as she wanted to concentrate on the official mission at hand.

Mousse and Frenchie took off together, as a flight of two, shortly before 8 PM with Mousse, the designated leader, in command. Their mission; patrol the night sky above the Strait of Hormuz and protect US Navy ships and civilian shipping transiting through the global choke point.

No one expected the Iranians to mount any serious aerial threat. Night combat stretched beyond the Islamic Iranian Air Force's known capabilities. Targets, if any, would be small boats attempting to harass ships funneled into the narrow strait. On a moonless night like this one, only radar could detect blacked-out Iranian craft, some no larger than a rigid-inflatable Zodiac. In the inky waters far below, a myriad of targets, large and small, appeared on the F-16's small radar screen. Discerning the Good Guys from the Bad Guys and both from the many more neutral civilians was a task neither Mousse nor Frenchie were equipped to do. They were briefed before take-off to expect guidance over the radio from a control authority should the need arise, preceded by a classified code word. The two fighter pilots did not know who this person or persons were or where they were. The intelligence officer conducting the pre-mission briefing declined to entertain questions on the sensitive subject.

"Theirs was not to question why. Theirs was to do or die." The line from Tennyson's poem, *Charge of the Light Brigade*, stuck in Mousse's consciousness like an earworm. If night combat reared its vicious head, the Peregrine missiles carried by each F-16 would be brought to bear. Their armament boasted dual-mode target seekers effective against both small boats and aircraft, as Frenchie demonstrated the previous week with his shoot-down of the Iranian MiG-29. Unlike their avian namesakes, the ne missiles could take surface prey and airborne targets alike. At least there was that.

While Mousse and Frenchie teamed up as a flight of two, the pair operated independently in the air. Instead of the duo taking the aerial playing field together, they functioned more like a pro wrestling tag team. One jet patrolled the assigned airspace while the other refueled from the tanker. Then they switched places, talking to the radar controller on the surface more often than they did to each other.

Boring holes in the night sky gave her more time to think. Most nights, the two pilots would bring iPods and listen to music through earbuds inserted under their helmets' earphones. Frenchie grooved on classic Cajun tunes, all sawing fiddles, lilting accordions, and raucous lyrics in Cajun French. Mousse usually got off on smooth jazz, but not tonight. Too many extraneous thoughts demanded her attention. Even the midnight sky's serenity presented no rival for the cacophony of competing ideas coursing through her mind.

Throughout her Air Force career, Mousse observed two cardinal commandants, which she adopted early on; no sex with married men and no romantic entanglements with fellow squadron members. Now, both crystal-clear principles had been shattered like dropped wine glasses. Her ideals fragmented into shards of shame, her shame. There was no shame for having recreational sex. Long ago she abandoned the teachings of her adolescence; that sex was for procreation only.

"I'm not a home-wrecker," she told herself. But even after rejecting married man Frenchie's clumsy approach in the chow hall, she then let the deal go down. Not merely let it happen, she had actively sought it out. bordering on seduction. Rationalization suggested to her

if Frenchie's marriage was rock-solid, he would not have propositioned her. No harm, no foul, her hormones and her longing told her.

A romantic intra-squadron relationship, one involving genuine, heart-felt feelings, could be problematic. A quick sport fuck was one thing, a love affair was something else. Tonight, as flight lead, she possessed the authority to send Frenchie into harm's way or to direct him back to home base and safety. What if they received a hot vector on the radio? Who would take the combat lead? Could she make a dispassionate tactical decision concerning a lover's life?

Did her wild encounter with Frenchie in the pool room kick-start a romance? The sex was delicious. Mousse was down with an occasional roll in the proverbial hay, a causal hook-up now and then, but the tenderness she craved had been absent during her tryst with the Cajun. Receiving him while nude and bent over a pool table had not been sweetly romantic, only totally orgasmic.

She could not deny her feelings for Frenchie. His sly smile, gentle southern manners, intelligence, wit, and Cajun accent were too much to ignore. Feeling remorseful, thoughtful even, about killing the Iranian pilot indicated there was more to Marcel Thibodeau than a self-centered remorseless fighter pilot. Did he and Mousse have a future together?

Her aircraft topped up with jet fuel, Mousse retarded the throttle a tiny fraction of an inch. The slight decrease in thrust allowed the tanker to move ahead of her. With nothing to show absolute speed, she saw only her position relative to larger aircraft. It looked to her like she backed out of the receiving position. Retracting and closing the open refueling slot, she instinctively clinched her thighs together on the ejection seat. Navigation lights extinguished, no need to advertise her presence, she turned the fighter toward the patrol area over the contested strait.

Long ago, the sexual analogy displayed in the aerial refueling process would have generated locker room humor on the radio between the tanker crew and the fighter pilot. But. such juvenile repartée had long been consigned to the dustbin of history.

That thought brought up the unseen elephant in the cramped cockpit, Bull Conner. His pressure to give in was relentless. If she wanted a promotion, the price was sex. If she went to the OSI, the price was a shit storm to endure. When or how, would it ever end?

It all started at the U. S. Air Force Academy. Comely, and some not so cute, female cadets were continually harassed by male upper classmen. Most women she knew at the "Blue Zoo," as they called the campus, experienced sexual pressure; unwanted touching, lewd jokes, crude come-ons. It never stopped. Common at civilian colleges, this rude behavior took greater significance when senior students held rank over underlings at a service academy. Still, she never gave in, but she also never complained up the chain of command. No sense in rocking the boat or the aircraft.

Once in a fighter squadron, for her the atmosphere improved and the air cleared somewhat. The squadron jocks were far more mature than cadets. Putting one's life in another's hands suggested caution to potential abusers. Often, the slings and arrows of harassment were unintentional or unconscious. Those she could shrug off. Conner was something else, a throwback sexual predator.

How he had gotten away with his antics for a 20-year career remained a mystery to his intended next mark.

Raised in a conservative religious family, Mousse rarely heard about sex growing up. The subject always came up in the context of making babies. Pleasure did not enter the equation. Sex outside marriage did not exist in polite company. Melissa Taylor, Captain USAF, had long ago left those mental constraints behind in various motel rooms and apartments, always of her own free will. The impasse with her squadron commander rang differently. Soon she would have to decide on a way forward, to either compromise her personal ethics or to harm her career.

She wanted that promotion on the road to commanding a squadron and she wanted it badly. Achieving her goal would set yet another example for girls and women to follow. Females had commanded squadrons and wings, so that glass ceiling was already shattered. Mousse intended to add another brick in the wall against misogyny. But to do that, she would have to give in to the worst sort of female stereotype; sex for hire. How to reconcile what she needed to do with what she knew to be wrong? Maybe it would be like the summer before formal entrance to the Academy. That was a burden to bear, like basic training. Constant harassment, nit-picking regulations, inspections, childish hazing. All designed to test how badly she wanted to be a cadet, how badly she wanted to be a U. S. Air Force officer, how badly she wanted to fly. Once endured, it could be dismissed.

Perhaps that was the way to look at the path ahead, a burden to be endured for a spell and then forgotten. An episode with Conner, get the performance appraisal in hand, then get on with her life. What was it they used to tell virgin Victorian brides? "Lay back and think of England." But what if the price was too high in terms of her self-esteem? Maybe she should just tell Conner no and let the proverbial chips fall where they may. Her self-image intact, she could fly jets, move on to a staff position and eventually retire never having achieved command. But Conner was not the type to take "No" for an answer and forget about it. He promised to retaliate. Squadron scuttlebutt held that Bull had contacts at the U. S. Air Force personnel center. A bad fitness report, a missed promotion, and her career advancement would be terminated. Telling Bull Conner to take a hike would be the honorable thing to do. Or get screwed, get promoted, and eventually command a squadron. Or have Conner wreck her career and serve out the remainder of the 20 years until retirement in obscurity. Not a decision one could flip a coin over.

With a full load of fuel and a long duration on station left in her mission, she had plenty of time to think and to decide which of the two rocky paths to take.

Chapter 9
King Khalid Air Base, Saudi Arabia

Two days later. Frenchie had never seen her so agitated. He had rarely seen her agitated at all, unless it was because of a flight member's screw-up. Melissa Taylor strode past him without speaking in the narrow corridor, her flight boots' footfalls echoing off the bare walls. Instead of her usual cheery greeting, she just nodded in recognition and continued along the hall toward the door leading into the squadron commander's office. Her face hard, her lips tight, and her eyes blazing blue under furrowed brows, she appeared to be a woman on a mission. But what mission and why was it so upsetting?

He waited a full minute after she closed the door behind her, then followed, letting himself into the outer office, quietly opening and closing the door. Two administrative assistants occupied the space, each behind her own desk. The two specialists were well known in the squadron for efficiently handling the necessary paperwork, for being friendly and outgoing as well. Among the male pilots, the two were famous as the best-looking enlisted troops in the squadron. They were hand-selected by Lieutenant Colonel Bull Conner to be his admin team.

On Frenchie's left sat a tall, statuesque Black woman, LaTonya Jefferson, hailing from Philadelphia, or as she put it, "South Philly." On his right sat a slashingly beautiful Latina, Miranda Lopez, from New Mexico, or as she referred to her home state, "God's country." The two seemed inordinately busy working away at their computers, staring at their screens with focused intent. Military protocol would ordinarily call for one or the other to greet an entering officer, but silence reigned, broken only by determined clattering on keyboards. Each woman pounded her keys, using undue force, with dual looks of complete detachment on their faces.

Frenchie stepped up to each, putting his index finger across his lips in the universal signal for quiet. Each woman nodded and continued typing loudly. He padded up to the commander's closed door, walking carefully to avoid footfalls in his clunky flying boots. Resting his ear on the thin, cheap portal to Conner's lair, he heard two voices emanating from the inner office, voices in turmoil, excited, emotional.

"You know what I want, what I need, and I know what you have to have." He could make out Conner's voice.

"Not here, not now, and maybe never," Mousse replied, her tone rising.

Frenchie sensed hurried footsteps, almost a scuffle. Someone approached the closed door from inside the office. Quickly snatching up a random stack of papers from a desk, he studied the top sheet as if it were the final exam in an English literature class. Melissa Taylor burst from the boss' cubicle, her face flushed, her flight suit unzipped to her bra. She rushed past Frenchie with no acknowledgement and exited, zipping up her uniform as she hurried past. The commander's door slammed behind her, followed by the outer door. He listened to her footsteps fade down the hall.

Frenchie thought about pursuing her, took two steps toward the exit, then hesitated, unsure of his next move. He stared back at the other two women with his palms upturned as if to say, "What the hell just happened?"

The pair peered at each other for a long while, expressions of knowing disgust playing across their faces. Both half-turned to Frenchie and repeated the "silence please" signal. They continued to stare at him. Did he detect subtle pleading? Was this a cry for help? Or were the two imploring him to leave and leave now? He elected to receive the third-choice signal and let himself out of the cubicle. As he started along the hall, the sound of determined typing again rang out, all without a word spoken.

Late that night, off the flying schedule for a change, Frenchie lay in his bunk staring toward the invisible ceiling above him in the dark. He was unable to sleep. At infrequent intervals, the scream of jet engines echoed through the night. Large, multi-engine planes emitted a throaty, long-lasting roar while fighters spoke in a sharper, higher-pitched voices which faded more quickly. He wished he was airborne himself, preoccupied with the mission at hand and not with the dilemma presented to him. The night sky's inherent isolation appealed to him. He longed to be under a canopy of diamond-bright stars with the night ground obscured far below. To be up where the air flowed cold and clear and pure, and so did the problems. Vexing aviation issues are addressed with increased afterburner thrust, a burst of 20mm cannon fire, or the dispatch of a Peregrine missile or two. This problem with Mousse was different.

Or was it even his problem? Mousse could handle herself. Maybe he should just butt out. He could not dismiss the haunted look on her face as she escaped from the commander's lair. His heart longed to reach out to her. Did she need or even desire his help? Would Mousse welcome his insertion into the dysfunctional dynamics between her and Bull? Thinking of insertion, what was his true motivation in this affair? Jealousy? A dated, old-school, desire to save a fair maiden in distress or just plain desire for said maiden, who showed him she was not a maiden at all. He glanced at his laptop on a tiny desk beside his bed. The screen remained blank, no alerts. No email from Yvette had arrived in what, two or three days? Why did he still care? Did she?

Fighter pilots are by profession problem solvers, accustomed to decisive action. They are singularly adept at addressing issues head on, canopy to canopy. But this situation was not that simple. It was not a matter of which weapon to use or what airborne maneuver to perform. It seemed to Frenchie ground-bound challenges involving other people, human emotions, and sexual tension did not lend themselves to kinetic solutions. Subtlety got him into Mousse in more ways than through enthusiastic sex. He found himself caring for her as a person, not only as an object of desire. Now, with that insight, her problems were his too, should he accept the self-assignment. Mousse had not asked for his involvement. She might even resent his interference.

Perhaps a direct approach to Conner would succeed, depending on what the definition of success Frenchie chose. Conner did not like Frenchie, he had made that clear, nothing to lose there. Maybe a mention of the OSI would cool Conner's jets. But the original question remained, should he engage at all?

An image came alive in his brain, unannounced, as if his mental software presented an analogy to him. He pictured himself flying his F-16 above a cloud deck, the solid undercast hiding what lay below. Over a break in the sheet of white, he saw an air battle taking place. The swirling mêlée once called a "dog fight" but now referred to as a "fur ball" raged, a change in nomenclature more vividly describing the metaphor of an actual canine confrontation. Same imagery, different terminology. Several friendly fighter planes were engaged with an equal number of Bad Guys. The combatants were adsorbed in their struggle, unaware of his presence above them. He could continue on his way as if he had never even seen the fight or he could push his throttle to the max and dive into the fray.

Viewed in this airborne light, Frenchie's path forward was clear to him. He would engage in the morning, joining the human relations fur ball.

Chapter 10
King Khalid Air Base, Saudi Arabia

Every morning at eight o'clock, 0800, Lieutenant Colonel "Bull" Conner attended the wing commander's daily briefing at wing headquarters. He tried to use the appearance to impress his immediate superior with his expertise and leadership qualities. Conner then returned to the squadron with an official prevue of the day's action on the air base.

Frenchie waited until 0815, then let himself into the squadron commander's outer office. The two administrative clerks looked up from their computers, then quickly pivoted back to their respective screens, not typing, but not ignoring Frenchie. He got right to the point.

"The scene yesterday with Captain Taylor, you two acted like that scenario was normal. What's up with that?" he asked.

The two women exchanged silent stares, as if each hoped the other would speak first.

"Captain Thibodeau, we don't want any trouble," LaTonya replied.

"You know this isn't right. You know what's going on between those two, don't you? You heard what I did. There will be trouble. Do you want to be part of the solution or part of the problem? My next stop can be the OSI. You need to tell me everything."

Sometimes silence is advisable, sometimes required, and sometimes the dam breaks and the truth pours out in an unfiltered torrent. Miranda took a deep breath and spoke first.

"Sir, what you saw is why we never let ourselves be alone with him. He's gone from accidental touching, to groping, to big-time pressure to come across."

"Why haven't you been to the OSI? It's their job to stop this crap," Frenchie replied, stating the obvious, for the second time in less than 48 hours.

"Yes sir, but the colonel said if we complained to anyone, he'd ruin our careers. The OSI office here is all-male. They'll never take the word of an enlisted troop over an officer." Miranda from God's Country spoke out forcefully.

LaTonya woman quickly chimed in, the words tumbling out of her mouth. She could not speak fast enough. Her South Philly accent ricocheted off the hard walls.

"I need this job. My baby's home in Philly with my mama and I'm their only support."

Miranda added, "What can the OSI do? That's just the way some men are. But not you, captain."

"Maybe I'll go to the OSI myself, I saw enough to file a report," Frenchie said. Alerting the OSI would mire him deeper in the coming sticky, smelly mess.

"If you do, the colonel will claim you're just a jilted lover. But if you make an official complaint, leave us out of it." Lopez made herself clear. She and LaTonya could take care of themselves.

***

At 1100, Frenchie returned to the outer office and in his best "command" voice, told the two clerks, "Time for you two to go to lunch." For better or worse, he had chosen to intrude into a situation where he had not been invited and was perhaps unwelcomed by the people affected.

The women stood and left the cubicle with dual, "Yes sirs."

Frenchie knocked on the squadron commander's door. From inside came, "Yeah, what is it?"

He entered, closed the door behind him, stood at attention, and rendered a snappy hand salute. Frenchie got the same feeling as when beginning an air-to-air engagement. The glazed doughnut he ate for breakfast pulled six Gs in the pit of his stomach. "Bull" Conner scanned some official paperwork scattered on his desk. He glanced up. "What do you want, captain?" he asked, then continued reading, head back down.

"It's about Captain Taylor, sir."

Conner looked up, his brows furrowed, his jaw clinched. He stared up at Frenchie. "OK, let's have it."

"I accidently overheard what went down in this office yesterday between you and her. It didn't sound good. I wanted, with all due respect sir, to hear your side of the story before I thought about going to the OSI."

"Captain Thibodeaux, if you get within 100 yards of the OSI office, I'll ruin your career, such that it is. I don't like you. Do you understand why? I'll tell you. You're one of those Cajun white trash people I grew up near. In East Texas, your people snuck across the border from Louisiana with your Cajun ways, your un-American language, and your weird French food. They tried to turn Texas into sorry-ass Louisiana by running down real Americans. White trash, that's what we called your kind. That's what you are, white trash."

"*Pourbelle blanche*," Anger rising, Frenchie translated, a service not well-received behind the desk as indicated by the look on the commander's pug face.

Conner continued on, "Don't get smart with me, captain. Now, get out of my office and if you're lucky, I'll forget this conversation ever happened."

Frenchie saluted; a courtesy not returned from behind the gray metal desk. He performed an about-face and left.

"You're banging her, aren't you?" were the last words coming from his squadron leader as the door shut behind him.

"Probably never again," Frenchie thought to himself. The encounter with Conner had gone as far south as possible. He had not previously grasped Bull's hatred of Cajuns. However, Conner perceived instinctively Frenchie's dilemma, and now Frenchie understood it too. Why did he beard the old lion in his own government-issued den? Was he trying to protect Mousse or keep her all to himself? Was his high-minded objection to sexual harassment founded on ethics or carnal desire? What was his next step? Unfortunately, that difficult decision was soon taken out of his hands.

Later in the afternoon, Frenchie checked the flying schedule, a whiteboard in the squadron operations center. He hoped for an extended night flight. Aviation always cleared his head and helped him to get his priorities straight. A black marker slash crossed out his name. Another pilot had taken his place. When he asked the officer behind the counter why he was no longer on the duty roster, the lieutenant looked away, unwilling to face Frenchie.

The junior officer stammered, "Orders, Frenchie," without revealing the origin of those orders.

Before he could investigate further, Chief Bichet motioned him aside.

"Captain Thibodeau, your assignment orders came through. Here are the required ten copies."

"Orders, what the hell? What orders?" "

You're going back to Arizona, to the training command. It's an administrative position on the wing staff. You're on the next charter flight out, the day after tomorrow."

Frenchie took the news like a right cross to the jaw. He was not due to rotate back to the States for another three months at the earliest. Why the rush with less than 24 hours until departure? A wing staff job, what did he do to deserve an assignment flying an earthbound desk? The senior sergeant stepped closer, head down, and in a barely audible voice spoke on, disclosing information.

"Captain, it didn't come from me, but Colonel Conner spent most of the afternoon on the phone back to the States, setting up this transfer. I think he has some serious dirt on an assignment officer at headquarters. I know he also has an asshole buddy on the wing staff at

Luke Air Force Base. Better get packing. You'll surprise your wife."

After a moment's pause, his heart racing, in a cold sweat, Frenchie hedged his bets to cover an eventuality which may or may not be forthcoming. He needed hard data if he was to retaliate.

"Chief, how about getting me the full names and social security numbers of the two admin clerks, Captain Taylor, and Colonel Conner?"

The chief master sergeant, who was not promoted to his exalted position by being unaware of what was going on in his squadron, looked sideways at the officer standing in front of him. He hesitated, took a deep breath, then spoke.

"Captain, I'm not supposed to give out that info, but I understand why you're asking. Are you sure you want to bring down a shit storm?"

"Thanks, Chief, I haven't decided what I'll do. Someone should do something. Those gals in the office are your people, they deserve help. Here's my stateside cell phone number in case they need it. Have you thought about going to the OSI yourself?"

"I get it, Captain. I'm less than six months from retirement. I don't need this on my way out to civilian life," the senior enlisted man said.

"Sorry Chief. Anyway, next time you're in the Crescent City, I'm good for a drink at Pat O'Brien's. Maybe a hurricane."

"Thanks captain, but those foo-foo drinks are too sweet for me, I'll take a Jack and water, light on the water. *Bonne chance et prendez-vous attention, sir.*"

***

He was throwing clothes into his duffel bag in his cramped, barren room when a staccato knock rattled his door. He opened it to find Melissa Taylor standing there, hands clenching her slender hips, a scowl distorting her pretty face.

What a pleasant surprise, Mousse. I've given the butler the night off, won't you come in?"

"No, I won't come in. You went to see Bull Conner, didn't you? You promised to keep quiet, but you got involved anyway. Did you think about making things worse?"

"Sorry Mousse, I'm just trying to help."

"Conner, thanks to you, can't back off now. His ego won't let him. I may never fulfill my dream of leading a squadron."

"Mousse, a dream without a plan is a hallucination," Frenchie said. It was not the most tactful reply he could have made.

The two pilots looked at each other for 10, 20, 30 seconds without speaking. Frenchie with arms crossed over his chest, Mousse squeezing her hips in defiance.

"Who says I don't have a plan?" She finally replied.

"Does your plan involve screwing Bull Conner?"

"Isn't that what a prostitute would do?"

With that, Mousse whirled around and marched off down the hall, disappearing from view and potentially from Frenchie's life forever. He slowly closed the door and leaned back against it, panting. When a die is cast, when a card is played, it is hard to perceive at the time if the move was the right one. Frenchie was almost certain now his choice to enter the sexual harassment fray had been the wrong one. After a deep sigh, he sat at his laptop, starting an email to Yvette announcing his unexpected return to marital bliss in Arizona. He hesitated, stopped short of hitting the send button, and shut down the computer.

That night, as on most recent nights when not flying, he again wished himself to be airborne despite the fighter jet process becoming increasingly less satisfying. Usually, he sought solace in the night sky, away from the ever-deepening morass involving Yvette, Mousse, and Bull Conner. But not lately, reality kept intruding into the cockpit's secure sanctuary. In an environment requiring intense focus, a moment's distraction could prove to be a serious, even fatal, mistake. He remembered other aviators who encountered similar problems concerning concentration. He asked himself, "How did they cope?"

Frenchie the teenager had devoured every book he could find on aviation, learning about the people who flew and who put their airborne adventures on paper. Written inspiration, adsorbed during his adolescence, did not include solutions to complications with the opposite gender. Laying wide awake in his none-too-comfortable bunk, his thoughts turned to the heroes of his youth.

He summoned in his mind's eye the poetic imagery spun effortlessly by expert story-tellers such as Count Antoine de Saint-Exupéry, Ernest K. Gann, and Richard S. Bach. They all flew at night and described the night sky's serenity, the beauty of unfiltered moonlight, and the cockpit's mothering comfort. Yet, each author/pilot suffered monumental problems in their lives. Their biographies told of tragedy, betrayal, and profound loss. How did they do it? How did they separate their domestic troubles from the satisfying airborne domain or vice versa? Why couldn't he do the same?

Was a dark cockpit, illuminated only by gages and stars, a comforting refuge, or a temporary artificial escape? Might the romance of nocturnal aviation offer unseen solutions to terrestrial entanglements? Who the hell knew?

Whatever the answer, Frenchie kept his faith in the skies' healing powers. However, the sky is not always benign. Sometimes death and destruction rain from the heavens.

CHAPTER 11
MORRO BAY, CALIFORNIA

The crows did not leave much, just some scattered scraps of broken eggshells, a few yolk stains on the sandy ledge, a lone black feather, and piles of stinky, white, bird crap. A single crow is no match for a peregrine. Even a small male falcon can more than defend himself from a crow attack by deploying superior flying skills and scalpel talons. But a peregrine defending his aerie and his eggs cannot prevail long over a whole murder of crows. As usual, the collective noun articulately described the actual action high on the cliff face.

The crows timed their well-planned assault perfectly. The female falcon was taking a break, flying inland to bathe in a shallow, fresh-water stream. Down in a narrow gully, splashing in the flowing wash, even her keen eyesight could not take in the sneak attack on her brood and on her mate.

The crows took turns swooping aggressively toward the male doing his incubation duty in the morning. Peregrines trade off hunting and sitting on their eggs.

Teamwork hatches their future offspring. The eggs arrived in late March, three buff-colored orbs with rust markings. Their patterns blended in with the rock-lined depression the female had scraped out in the cliff ledge's rear recess.

Peregrines can kill single predators as large as a bald eagle when the falcons are defending a clutch of eggs or hatchlings. Once the male took the crows' bait and launched off the cliff face, the fight ended—advantage crows. The corvids, with coordinated attacks, drove the male further and further away from the aerie until the rest of the murder could harvest the now-abandoned eggs. The male seemed strangely lethargic and unaggressive in defending his brood. Perhaps the crows sensed this. Crows are very perceptive and intelligent. A crow can count to at least ten, and the difference between one and two falcon nest defenders appeared obvious to members of the murder. Ordinarily, the falcon would experience only minor trouble dispersing a squadron of crows, but not this time.

Arriving back at the rudimentary nest, she found her mate perched on the ledge, staring out to sea. His wings drooped, trailing in the sand. Whether from fatigue, from battling the crows, from dejection at losing the clutch to the robbers, or something else; it was hard to discern. She landed beside him and hopped around the aerie, convincing herself the eggs were truly gone or smashed. Then, she too remained still, her feathers rippling in the ocean breeze. The raid had come too late in the breeding season to try again. There would be no chicks nor fledglings this year for the peregrine pair.

CHAPTER 12
KING KHALID AIR BASE, SAUDI ARABIA

Mousse stopped in front of Frenchie's door and paused, her fist poised to knock, then she hesitated. *Do I really want to do this? Should I really be doing this?* She asked herself two questions she already knew the answer to. For the past day, she had been regretting chewing Frenchie out over his confrontation with Bull Conner and for hurling the word "prostitute" back in his face. The dude was just trying to help, in his own inept way, whether or not he had been asked to get involved. Help he did not, get involved he did. Now there was an opportunity to disengage Frenchie from a situation in which he was not needed. Frenchie's sudden and unexpected transfer offered him, and Mousse, respite.

She looked up and down the corridor. No one coming. At first, she intended to knock softly so as to not waken anyone, it was after midnight, and to not announce her presence at Frenchie's door to prying eyes and ears.

She thought better of the stealth approach and rapped briskly on the thin, prefab door. After a few seconds, Frenchie opened the door in his boxers and a white tee shirt with *Louisiana State University—Geaux Tigers!* In violet and gold across the front. She expected him to appear sleepy at this hour, but the Cajun was obviously wide awake and had been for some time as shown by red his eyes.

Before he could speak, she stepped inside and closed the door behind her. For once, he had no wisecrack at her appearance at his room.

"Mouse. What the hell?" was all he could stammer out.

"Frenchie, we need to talk," she started off with a cliché. "Or rather, I need to talk and you need to listen." That set the verbal stage.

She sat down on his unmade bed, uninvited, and Frenchie plopped down at his plastic desk chair, waiting for her to speak. The only light in the room came from the reading light on his desk, a cone of white. Mousse slowly crossed her legs in the semi-darkness.

I burned your ass yesterday for going, without being asked, to Conner. I was upset that you jumped into a problem not of your doing. Yes, you did make things worse, but you were trying to help. I understand that and I appreciate your efforts."

Mousse had that look in her eyes, the look she flashed when debriefing a flight which had not gone according to plan, one in which a wingman or two had screwed up. Her voice was slow, her speech was measured, the words carefully chosen, the tone not high pitched or shrill. But behind the language was steel. She went on.

"I can handle this. If I give in to Conner is my decision and mine alone. I will keep you informed, if you wish. If I need you to go to the OSI, I'll ask."

She pulled a 5x7 card from the mounded breast pocket of her flight suit and handed it across the room to Frenchie.

"Here is my cell phone number for texts and my personal email handle. If you want to keep in touch, I'll need yours. I'm not in the habit of exchanging contact info with married men, but this time I will."

Frenchie looked at her for the longest time, as if deciding what to do.

"I don't know how much longer, or if, I'll be a married man."

That Rubicon having been crossed; Frenchie went on. He told of how Yvette's communication had been increasingly infrequent and disjointed, with shallow messages poorly composed in obvious haste. He related how he felt his wife slipping away and how his reaction to that puzzled him.

"Do you still love her?" Mousse asked.

"I don't know. Maybe this transfer will let me figure it out in person instead of by email."

Frenchie scribbled his contact data on a half sheet of paper and handed it over to her.

"Watch out for yourself Mousse, check six at all times." He added the classic fighter pilot's words of caution--look behind you for any approaching unseen threat. "Also, I need to tell you I care for you," he added, his voice catching with emotion.

Mousse, stood up, taking the two steps to the door, passing the still-seated Frenchie. She reached for the handle and grasped it, pausing for long seconds. She knew well sometimes action is taken after much thought, after gaming all the possible outcomes, after considering the knowable pluses and minuses. Her visit to his room this night followed that careful scenario. But sometimes things just happen and decisions are only gut-felt. *Sometimes,* she thought, *you just live for the moment.* Slowly she let her fingers slide off the door lever and pressed the lock button with a firm click. Reaching over the desk, Mousse switched off the light.

CHAPTER 13
PHOENIX, ARIZONA

The budget, bare-bones rental car crept through the winding residential streets of a Phoenix suburb, past Identikit tract houses, each more or less indistinguishable from its neighbors. Pitch dark at one o'clock in the morning, scattered street lights strove in vain to dispel the gloom. Their feeble amber glow was attenuated, even choked, by shoals of blowing brown dust driven by a blistering hot wind. A *haboob,* a desert sandstorm, started streaming across the flat Arizona plain in the afternoon and continued to gain strength after sunset. Surrounding the subdivision, bare fields, bone dry and uncultivated, added their precious topsoil to the mix. Above, the usually bright stars were invisible. The car's headlights struggled to penetrate the swirling, churning, airborne sand. Obscuration in darkness made it difficult to get a sense of the street layout. Almost lost, the driver peered into the night as if getting closer to the windshield might help him penetrate the gloom.

The howling storm, the lack of visible stars, and the coming confrontation with cold hard truth disquieted Frenchie. His hands shook on the plastic steering wheel. His mood improved when he could see the sky, day or night, but tonight this solace was unavailable to him. He worried about not notifying his wife of his premature return. Intuition told him to learn the facts concerning her ever-increasing emotional detachment, he needed to arrive unannounced. He wondered if she still slipped into bed nude. He wondered if she still slept alone. He wondered if he still cared, and if so, why.

The night displayed all the visceral atmospherics of a nocturnal combat mission conducted in rotten weather. Before any aerial action began, he always experienced the familiar 6G doughnut deep in the pit of his stomach. Tonight's sortie in Arizona pulsed with similar anticipation, with the stirring action poised to begin. In combat, aggressive maneuvering would erase the unease generated by the preliminaries. A twisting, turning dog fight, or fur ball, required pulling real Gs instead of a false, doughnut-induced sugar-high reaction. Physical exertion settles mental matters and stomachs alike. Adrenaline trumps pure cane sugar. Tonight's events might not be as straightforward as a combat sortie with as clear an outcome. Frenchie knew and dreaded what was to come.

If he was wrong about his souring relationship with Yvette, a joyful reunion awaited him. The mutual strains of absence would vanish in a frenzy of discarded clothes followed by uninhibited sex. However, if his suspicions proved validated, a new, uncharted course lay ahead into his future, into a fresh life. A life without his wife.

Frenchie cut the headlights on his econobox car. He coasted to a stop on the suburban street, across from his house, across from their house. The neighborhood was gloomy, illuminated by only a single amber lamp on a post at a nearby intersection and from swirling reflections off the blowing dust clouds.

He spotted two vehicles in his driveway. Neither one was Yvette's SUV; that was probably in the garage. He strained to see if his Corvette slept there under its silver cover, mothballed, awaiting his return from deployment. The sleeping sports car remained in place, but hidden in the shadow of a hulking truck. The black pickup boasted over-sized knobby tires, an exhaust the size of a sewer pipe, and a chromed roll bar standing erect and proud in the bed. He suspected that it had been there before. All the house lights appeared extinguished, save a dim glow emanating from the upstairs bedroom window, a pulsing pale light, the flickering of a candle.

Frenchie started the car, lights off, and pulled away from the curb, away from his tract house, away from his marriage, and away from Yvette. Without looking back, he drove off into the night, more alone than he had ever been.

The city lights of Phoenix blurred in his eyes while he traced his way to the air base, to the unmarried officers' temporary quarters. While driving, he ruminated on how and why the hell it had all gone wrong. Love flowed sincerely between them early in their union. There were the getaway trips to New Orleans, a romantic week in Paris (the Parisians understood only a few words of their Cajun French patois. Given the residents of the French capital attitude toward what they consider to be incorrect French, could their confusion been contrived?). No matter, the week's goal was uninhibited love-making. Mission accomplished.

The constant, re-occurring deployments took a toll on both partners. It seemed he was absent as much as he was at home. When he returned to Yvette, each time he found it harder to connect emotionally like they achieved prior to him leaving. Without a shared life, they grew apart. Every return became more awkward until all that remained in their relationship was the physical interplay releasing sexual tension.

Could they put things back together after mutual infidelity? His dalliance with Mousse was more than a casual affair and one he was not willing to give up. He still ached for her. Yvette's increasing detachment indicated that she too had found someone new. No, now it was finished. Once shattered, love and dedication cannot be re-assembled easily.

What survived of their marriage would be subject to painful legalisms, the division of belongings, and a halting start to an uncharted chapter in his life.

He slipped off his wedding ring, recently re-installed on his left hand, rolled down the driver's side window, and hurled the gold band out into the blowing dust. The wind carried it away like the remnants of his union. It looked to be an interminable night, storm or no storm. Sleep did not beckon.

Culmination of the slow-motion break-up with Yvette represented a new category of challenge for Frenchie, one lacking a simple, quick solution. Like all fighter pilots, he became accustomed to solving issues quickly with instant feedback. Bombs either hit or missed their targets. An air-to-air engagement ended when he ran out of missiles or ran low on fuel. A post-mission debriefing settled the doubts, clearing the symbolic air for another day, another sortie.

Things painted themselves stark black and pristine white in the world of fighter planes, but showed shades of mottled gray and confusion reigned in the domestic domain. He had lost Yvette and left Mousse behind in another desert.

At least he would have plenty of time to sort matters out, to plan his next step, while flying his gray steel desk buried in the bureaucratic bowels of wing headquarters.

Unfortunately, there is more than one way to lose a spouse than through drawn-out emotional distancing. Sometimes the rupture is sudden and unexpected.

CHAPTER 14
MORRO BAY, CALIFORNIA

His landing was more like a semi-controlled crash than a carefully executed touchdown. The male peregrine arrived back at the aerie on Morro Rock with a thud in a pile of disarranged feathers. Shaking himself and squawking, he stood unsteadily on his once-sturdy legs and looked repeatedly left and right out over the bay. His wings drooped, their trailing edges with his long flight feathers dragged behind him in the red dust of their mutual home. The female watched her mate of four years closely. She had never seen him ill like this. By morning, he was dead. The darkness came for him deep in the night.

As dawn slowly lit the rocky recess, she could make out his body, lying in a heap near the cliff's edge. One motionless wing tip protruded up, as if reaching for the sky for the last time. His black saucer eyes, ever bright and shining, were now dull and lifeless. The female chirped and squawked as she hopped around his carcass, urging him to awaken, to live, to fly again. After ten minutes, she gave up the effort and starred out to sea, seeing nothing but gathering clouds. At last, she pushed off the ledge, spread her broad wings, and flew away, not looking back. She would not return until the vultures and crows cleaned up the mess.

Deep in the dead falcon's crop, the sack in his gullet where his food, meat, was prepared for digestion, lay a single lead shot the size of a tiny pea. Indigestible, the pellet leached its poisonous lead into his bloodstream and corrupted his central nervous system, eventually killing him, slowly. Source for the poison was the ring-necked dove the paired falcons shared. The dove had been shot, crippled but still able to fly, by a rebellious hunter.

The state of California outlawed lead shot because of its deadly effect on condors, vultures, and other scavengers who feasted on carcasses containing the pellets. Non-toxic pellets replaced the lead for sale throughout the state. Even so, rarely would a raptor, who prefer live prey, ingest the poisonous pills. But no one can forecast where a single bit of lead can pop up in the food chain.

The hunter who shot at the dove knew about the total lead shot ban, but cared not a damn. Some outdoor people disdain government interference in, and regulation of, activities they consider a God-given birthright, like bird hunting. The hunter's refusal to follow common sense and the law resulted in the peregrine male's death and the dispatch of his mate from her rocky haven. Sadly, the renegade hunter never knew of the avian destruction he caused. Though, if he had known, chances are he would not have cared in the least. What's a few more dead birds when you are making a statement protesting perceived political overreach?

A few miles south of Morro Bay, past other beach cities, despite the popular impression of an over-crowded coast, California becomes wild and desolate. Here, the shore land is all but uninhabited by humans. The few beaches are deserted. Hills are covered in scrub, not houses. It is the domain of the sea otter, the bobcat, the raccoon, the bear, the mountain lion, and now, a lone peregrine falcon. The solitary bird flew along the coast, paralleling the surf, alternately stroking the air and riding the breeze. She had lost her brood, her mate, and her home. Each would be hard to replace.

CHAPTER 15
LUKE AIR FORCE BASE, PHOENIX, ARIZONA

"Where are those efficiency reports?" the older officer asked. "I need those files on my desktop by tomorrow morning."

The Chief of Aircraft Maintenance, a full colonel, stood, hands on hips, in the doorway of Frenchie's tiny, austere office.

"Sir, I'll send them when they're done. I'm sure you want a quality product. That process can't be rushed," Frenchie replied.

"Captain, Bull Conner warned me about you. If you want to get back to a squadron, to a flying billet, you'd better get with the program. Understood?"

"Yes sir, it's all perfectly clear. I'll get right on it."

The colonel turned and left without another word, leaving Frenchie alone to enjoy his fresh official digs. Four windowless walls painted a drab shade of light green, a battered desk, a swivel chair on castors (one broken), and a computer two generations out of date. That was it. The previous denizen taped travel posters on the blank walls, but she took them with her when transferred leaving the room devoid of any human element.

Frenchie checked his personal email account and his phone. Nothing from Mousse. Contact with her in the desert had been regular. The remote communication was always about squadron gossip, greetings from Chief Bichet, and the weather. Flight operations were discussed only in passing due to security concerns. No mention of Bull Conner and the fateful choice Mousse faced. Two weeks ago, the constant line of chat stopped. His texts went unanswered. Email disappeared into cyberspace. He had access to the operational and safety network, he knew there had been no accidents or combat losses, always a possibility with fighter pilots. There was nothing he could do.

Frenchie pushed his chair back, propped his flying, or more accurately, his non-flying boots, on his desk, and opened the latest copy of the Air Force Times. The bi-weekly newspaper's current edition featured on its front page the headline; *Promotions to Major Announced.*

A quick scan revealed the name he looked for, the one he hoped not to find. But there it was, "Melissa A. Taylor." Mousse stood out on the list. They would promote her to the rank of major in the United States Air Force during the coming year.

He tore the page displaying the names of newly minted majors from the newspaper and wadded it into a neat ball. His high angle basketball shot glanced off two corner walls, swished into the bin, nothing but net.

Crumpled newsprint disappeared into the battered government-issued wastebasket, never to be seen again.

He felt a profound sense of loss like something, or someone, important was missing from his life. She had made her choice and had chosen not to share it with him. That hurt.

One of Frenchie's pastimes, an activity he relished, watching classic movies, often brought back memories, memories of his own life mirrored on the screen. Recently, he viewed *The Thomas Crown Affair*. One scene launched off his computer and into his consciousness like a Peregrine missile homing in on his flailing psyche. During a chess match masquerading as foreplay, Faye Dunaway caressed the miter on Steve McQueen's bishop chessman. She slowly, seductively ran her fingertips down the piece's ivory tip. Images of the memorable pool room tryst with Mousse came flooding back. Frenchie had slammed down the laptop's cover, terminating the movie before the following steamy sex scene.

"How can you miss someone you never even knew well?" he mused. Two episodes of crazed coupling did not substitute for getting to know her as a person. All their interactions were superficial, even the carnal knowledge. What did she hold dear? What did she want out of life, other than the command of a squadron? Why the burning urge to lead an unruly group of fighter pilots? Where was she now? Who was she with?

He was forced to consider the eternal conundrum between the genders. Can hot sex and burning desire lead to emotional intimacy or should deep personal intimacy be rewarded with sex? Whatever the answer, he had failed with Mousse and now he was alone.

Sometimes you only get one chance at success, one shot at the basket. If the opportunity is not grasped, the prize slips past your palms. He ached to wrap his fingers around her silky smooth, firm buns and to look deep into her eyes, but that pleasure seemed to be out of reach. His hands hung empty, useless. Mousse was to be a major, the next step to commanding a squadron. She only did what she had to do. Bull Conner won this round. Would there be a rematch? Should there be?

Conner would continue to play his sexual baiting games until someone stopped him. Frenchie could take on the onerous task, but at what cost? He leaned farther back in his rickety office chair and stared up at the ceiling. Not for the first time, Frenchie envisioned the unfolding situation in aeronautical terms, a familiar coping mechanism for him. With closed eyes he saw himself flying his prized F-16. Spotting a large formation of enemy aircraft, loaded with bombs, on a course toward his home base, he follows them. On a steady heading, the Bad Guys have not spotted his small jet high above them.

Two forks in his imaginary aerial road presented themselves. He might shadow the Bad Guys, radioing an alert, hoping the base can mount a defense before destruction falls from the sky. He would probably survive this plan if enacted, but the base would get clobbered. Or, he could engage the far more numerous enemies after transmitting a wake-up call to the base. A determined attack would disrupt their carefully planned raid, giving the Good Guys time to mount a defense. In this scenario, the airbase survived. But Frenchie's odds of returning to that base would be slim-to-none after tangling with enraged and powerful foes.

Major life decision points are rarely obvious at the point they are taken. Far too often, the fork in the road becomes apparent only in hindsight, long after a course has been chosen for good or ill. For once, Frenchie sensed he now paused at such an important crossroads. The choice confronting him would set the progress of his Air Force career, his life, his future.

If he focused on the required but boring reports; he would make the colonel happy. If he kept his mouth shut about the sexual harassment occurring downrange in the Arabian desert, he might return to a flying squadron. That would put him back into the F-16 and into the sky, flying once again. He would then get on with his alternative life, perhaps with Major Melissa if she ever responded to his messages. Or he might try to piece a marriage back together with the luscious Yvette. That path seemed closed. Conversations with Yvette had gone nowhere, she was enamored with her new lover and kept steering the discussions back to a probable split.

The other fork in the road led straight off a metaphorical cliff. He could try to bring much-needed OSI attention to the sordid actions of Bull Conner. This course would bring down the shit storm Chief Bichet warned him of. Who knew what trouble Conner might stir up?

Melissa might have to surrender the promotion she wanted so much, that she gave so much of herself for. Undoubtedly, his life would be drastically altered on this alternate path and not for the better. Down this road, the Air Force would be better off. The military world would be cleansed from a sexual predator. Frenchie could revenge himself on Conner if he took this path. But what action would he be repaying? Conner's abuse of his rank or the loss of Mousse by Frenchie? Did it matter? She had not wanted his help, had not asked that he go to the OSI. If he did, his current nonexistent relationship with Mousse would never be repaired.

He believed in the United States Air Force. The service had become his life. He also believed in honor, duty, and fair dealing despite his occasional infidelity. He believed in not violating a military code of conduct, in not besmirching one's rank by forcing, or giving, sex for promotion. Frenchie recalled a line from another old film, *A man's gotta do what a man's gotta do*. Who said it? Who knows? Perhaps a young Clint Eastwood.

In his mind's eye, Frenchie banked his imaginary fighter plane's pointed nose toward the oncoming enemy formation, a gaggle led by Bull Conner. He pushed up the notional throttle, his decision made.

Marcel Thibodeau, Captain, United States Air Force, took out his phone, looked up two numbers and placed two calls. The first went to the Phoenix regional OSI office. The second to a local divorce lawyer whose number he got, just in case, from an ex-squadron member. This legal beagle offered a discounted fee for members of affinity groups such as split-prone military units. Business was excellent for the attorney, but he scheduled an appointment anyway. The call to the OSI agent was less immediately successful. The agent answering the phone was professionally non-committal, promised to respond, but offered no further details. Frenchie was committed. Now, the outcome of the fur ball engagement was only somewhat in his hands.

CHAPTER 16
KING KHALID AIR BASE, SAUDI ARABIA

Mousse, her assigned time on her aerial station expired, reduced power on the F-16's engine and pointed the aircraft's cobra-like nose toward her temporary home base in the desert. She began a long, gliding descent to land. As usual, the late nighttime patrol was uneventful, routine, boring. Normally, she would have requested to fly a few daytime sorties to maintain proficiency in other combat missions. However, lately she dedicated herself solely to night flying, avoiding as many of her squadron mates as possible, particularly the commander, Bull Conner.

No other pilots enjoyed droning sorties long after midnight. Her determined volunteering to fly in the desert dark was welcomed, if not understood, by her fellow Fighting Falcon drivers. Flying in the dark became her passion only after her sordid session with their much-unloved commander.

The hangover had been epic. She felt so awful the next morning, her hair hurt. Chief Bichet was not the only one with a secret supply of alcohol. Bull Conner's quarters were well stocked with illicit booze. He ushered her in with a beer and a smirking leer. Once the beer was consumed, she started downing gin on the rocks and lots of it. When the drinks finally hit her, their effect almost put her out. Intoxication limited her capacity to take part in the sex acts or to resist. Even so, she could understand what was happening to her. Later, Bull's grinning presence haunted her dreams. In her shaky memory, it seemed his aim had not been mere sexual pleasure, but domination. Or subjugation. Whatever his goals, she gave in drunkenly to his pressure, his desires, his fantasies.

The next morning, a long, hot shower did nothing for her aching head and even less for her body. She felt bruised all over, despite finding no marks anywhere on her. The mental contamination was far worse, having crawled under her skin, and no scrubbing washed it away. Many showers in the days and nights following dried out her smooth skin, leaving it red and raw. Three drenching, steaming torrents a day with US government-issued soap and towels will do that.

While the reoccurring night flights kept her out of sight from the rest of the squadron and of Conner, they did nothing for her peace of mind. Most pilots soon learn to resonate with the nighttime sky's emptiness. A few go on to write classics of aviation literature. Poets find it serene up there, to be alone with one's thoughts. Aye, but there lies the rub. Her thoughts, her memories, left the ground with her and stayed with her while airborne. The F-16 was no longer a secure cocoon of aluminum, plexiglass, and wind rush, lined with lighted gages, glowing radar displays, and illuminated switches. The Falcon's cockpit became a cramped prison cell for Mousse. She could not escape her deep sense of shame, no matter how long or how high she flew. In the days serving as her nights, her bed dreams became nightmares. Unafraid in a fighter cockpit, she had given in to a subconscious fear of failure, specifically the failure to be promoted. She grasped for cold, bronze leaves, the brass leaves of a major's rank. Even worse, she lacked the courage to report Conner's proposed bargain to the OSI. It was the right, the honorable thing to do. But she did not do it. Now it was too late.

She envied the actual falcons she saw in the desert day skies of Saudi Arabia. They flew when and where they wished with no worries, no memories, and their sex lives were theirs alone to enjoy. During her college education at the US Air Force Academy, Melissa assisted with the military school's mascots, an eyrie of falcons. She loved watching the birds fly and dreamed of doing so herself. After pilot training, when her assignment to the F-16 came through, she was pumped. To fly a fighter plane with the nickname of her avian charges was a wish fulfilled. However, the official name "Fighting Falcon" is never uttered by F-16 jocks. The pilot community much prefers "Viper" a moniker awarded due to the aircraft's reptilian, cobra-like profile, particularly when seen from nose-on. However, cobras are not vipers, a fine distinction lost on fighter pilots. Indeed, Mousse's call radio sign on this flight was "Viper One."

Looking back with the improved judgement of hindsight, she was forced to admit her envy of the tame academy falcons had been superficial. Yes, they flew, but they were never free. They always returned to a safe and predictable captivity. She now knew how those un-free birds felt, trapped in a world not of their making, ignorant of the greater world outside their manufactured eyrie. Mousse was now trapped in her own cage, like the non-fighting falcons of the Air Force Academy. The f-16 Fighting Falcon, the Viper, she piloted could not take her away from the mental captivity she and Bull Conner had constructed around herself.

Ahead, through the sloped windscreen, she spotted the airfield's lights shimmering in the growing dusty gloom. Dawn was breaking over Saudi Arabia. Its coming heat would burn away those things which happened in the night. Contacting the control tower, she received clearance to land. "I wonder if Conner will be at the squadron this early? He might stop by on his way to Wing Headquarters," she asked herself. She slowed the aircraft to prepare for touchdown. "Maybe if I dawdle in the intelligence shop, I'll miss him, he never goes there."

The airplane floated over the white numbers painted on the runway identifying it followed by the broad white stripes on the black asphalt background. Known as the "piano keys" the display is intended to aid depth perception. She raised the nose a few degrees to slow the plane further and to establish the right touchdown attitude. Like a peregrine falcon with its wings spread wide and legs extended, reaching for its aerie, the F-16 sank cautiously toward mother earth.

All hell broke loose. "Whoop! Whoop!" sounded in her earphones. Warning lights flashed in the cockpit and on the Head Up Display. The control tower came on the air insistently, "Viper One, go around! Repeat, go around!" The mobile control tower, a glass hut at the end of the runway staffed by a squadron pilot, fired a red flare across her flight path. Obeying the cacophony of dire warnings, she rammed the throttle full forward into the afterburner range and experienced the familiar push in the back. Airspeed built rapidly, driven by the thundering engine. She kept the nose on the horizon until she climbed several hundred feet, then glanced at the warning lights in the cockpit, now extinguished. The landing gear remained locked up, the wheels retracted. Distracted by her internal conflict, she had forgotten to lower the gear, and had been about to touch down on the aircraft's vulnerable belly.

Some airplanes can land on their bellies with minimum damage, mainly to replaceable sheet metal. Fighters cannot. Touch the ground with an F-16's fuselage and it will, as the old drinking song goes, "Tumble and roll and dig a big hole." It is rarely a survivable mistake. Mousse reentered the traffic pattern and triple-checked the landing gear. Three green lights showed the wheels properly down and locked long before touchdown.

After debriefing the intelligence troops concerning the night's non-events in the patrol area, she endured a very one-sided conversation in the squadron operations center. The Supervisor Of Flying, the SOF, a senior instructor pilot on duty overseeing flight operations stopped her. He read her the proverbial riot act referencing flight safety. Only her sterling reputation as an expert fighter pilot saved her from being written up for a serious safety violation. Mousse had been a scant few feet from lighting up the desert dawn with a fatal fireball lit on the runway.

As she left the ops center, she looked back to observe the SOF, a lieutenant colonel, conducting an intense conversation with Chief Bichet. The two senior officials from different worlds, officers and enlisted troops, stood apart from the rest of the room. In a corner, they huddled, their heads close together, their voices low. Animated, the SOF waved his hands, as pilots are wont to do, demonstrating the potential accident. Chief Bichet replied, his hands in his pockets, his eyes downcast.

By the time she finished the debriefings, the cooks were serving breakfast in the chow hall. Sitting alone, as usual, she picked at her plate of creamed chipped beef on toast. It was comprised of browned ground beef and cream gravy, mixed and spread over two slices of toasted white bread. The beige and white mess has been known to generations of military personnel, since World War II, as "SOS." short for "Shit On a Shingle." Not even the addition of fresh scrambled eggs on top saved the morning meal or stimulated her appetite.

Mousse looked up to find Chief Bichet standing over her, his benign bulk casting a shadow on her tray.

"Captain Taylor, might I have a word with you, *un bon mot?*"

"Sure chief, take a load off."

The senior enlisted man, nobody's fool, pulled up a plastic chair across the table from her and leaned in close to talk. The chow hall's background din would keep their conversation private. He placed an enormous bottle of Tabasco sauce next to her plate providing cover for the meeting in case anyone watched.

"Captain, this red stuff might help the SOS. You know, I've got an old-time buddy in the personnel section at headquarters, another Creole like me. She feeds me the straight skinny. I checked. Word has it you are on the next major's promotion board. The list appears in the *Air Force Times* next week. Your first salute as a major will come from me."

Mousse's scrubbed-red face showed no emotion at the news. The chief's expression never changed either. It was as if he expected the reaction he got, or rather did not get. He went on, sliding an official-looking piece of paper across the table to her.

"Here's an appointment slip with the flight surgeon. You're due at his clinic at 0900 today, better eat up, can't meet the doc on an empty stomach."

"I didn't make an appointment."

"No, the SOF made one for you. He pulled some strings to get you in ASAP."

"I don't need to see any quack and I'm off duty now," Mouse complained.

"With all due respect captain, the SOF told me to inform you this is not a request. It's either the doc or a flight safety write-up."

The chief stood up and left without a further word. None were needed. Tabasco did not improve the SOS.

Flight surgeons are medical doctors with special training in aviation medicine. They are educated on the stresses aerial flight imposes on the body and psyche. Each is assigned to a squadron as the aircrew's personal physician. A few are ex-pilots who found aviation insufficiently challenging in an operator's role and enrolled in medical school. All flight surgeons are required to fly occasionally to experience what they are treating. One medical task they seldom perform is actual surgery. The title "surgeon" stems from a long-ago time when military doctors primarily were surgeons, amputating battle-shattered limbs hence the common call sign, "Sawbones" hung on flight surgeons.

Mousse entered the exam room to find a senior nurse and the commander of the hospital, a full colonel, waiting. The colonel wore pilot wings below his flight surgeon's badge. His presence in the exam room was highly unusual. Full colonel flight surgeons almost never treat patients, being too busy with management, planning, adminstrivia, and whatever else it is that colonels do. The SOF must have exercised some serious clout to get the head doc involved. Either that or a covert oral report from Chief Bichet which got the clinic commander's attention.

The colonel waited and watched while the nurse took Mousse's vital signs, comparing the readings to her medical file stored on a laptop. Temperature, pulse rate, blood pressure, all were in the high range of normal. Weight down seven pounds. Height unchanged. The nurse, now serving as a chaperone, took exam notes on the laptop. The colonel, an avuncular older gentleman with a well-earned reputation for having seen it all, spoke up.

"Have a seat, Mousse. How are you doing?"

"OK, I guess."

The senior doc handed her a mirror, a round piece of glass with a foot-long handle. He faced the mirror toward her.

"What do you see?"

Mouse took the mirror, holding it up in front of her face, the first time in weeks she looked in a mirror at herself. It did not go well. Her hand on the handle quivered, shaking, blurring the reflected image. She traded hands with no improvement in steadiness. Overhead, the exam room's spotlight shone in the mirror, its reflection a bright splash on the wall behind her. The lighted spot danced over the wall like a berserk firefly despite her efforts to quell the shaking.

Gently, the colonel took the looking glass from her hand and asked again, "What did you see?"

"Me?"

"I see a person, an aircrew member, under extreme pressure. I've witnessed this syndrome during heavy combat operations. Circles under the eyes, hollow cheeks, weight loss. The symptoms all fit except for the abraded skin. Typically, the outcome is never good unless we address the source of the stress. I've flown with you, Mousse, you're good. But today, you tried to kill yourself. If this pattern keeps up without intervention, you'll succeed. I learned from your file your annual flight physical exam is nearly due. I'm entering on your record a preliminary diagnosis of Post-Traumatic Stress Disorder, PTSD. I'm grounding you and sending you back to the states for your exam. There's a charter flight in a few days and you'll be on it."

"Doc, I don't need to be grounded, don't want to be. I'll sort things out."

"Captain Taylor, this is not a matter for discussion. If you went out and killed yourself, I'd feel terrible. It's my responsibility to keep our aircrews safe. I don't know the source of your problems, but I have my suspicions. At the hospital in Texas, they have more resources to treat you. You can apply for flight status after your physical, if they clear you. In the meantime, enjoy the time off. Take care, Mousse."

The colonel and nurse rose as one and let themselves out of the examination room, leaving Mousse alone. As she left, without speaking, the nurse handed her a box of tissues. A few were drenched with salty tears before Mousse followed them.

Grounded pilots are always assigned to perform additional duties no one else wants to do, such as sitting in the mobile control tower, "Mobile," to prevent gear up landings. After her third daily stint in Mobile, Mouse returned to the squadron to find Chief Bichet looking for her. He drew her aside and in a low growl delivered unexpected news.

"Captain Taylor, there's a person waiting in my office to speak with you, now. Keep this under your hat, please mam. The bosses will get briefed soon enough."

The chief's office measured one-half the size of the commander's but was more tastefully decorated. Past posters from the New Orleans Jazz & Heritage Festival adorned the windowless cubicle's walls. A battered desk faced away from the entrance. Visitors were greeted by the chief turning around to be face-to-face with them, no official furniture in the way. The cluttered work surface featured an array of pictures of his smiling wife, grinning kids' school pictures, and a panorama of the NOLA French Quarter. Mousse let herself in and closed the door behind her. It clicked softly, closing off the space from the outside word. At the desk sat a Black woman in casual civilian clothes. The stranger stood, introduced herself, and handed Mousse a brown leather folder containing a US Government ID card stating her name, but with no rank noted. With the card was a gold badge with the words. "Special Agent" engraved in blue across the top. The special agent spoke first.

"Captain Taylor, I'm with the OSI. I need to interview you."

CHAPTER 17
LUKE AIR FORCE BASE, PHOENIX, ARIZONA

The OSI agent, a young Latino, sported business casual civilian clothes and asked to be addressed as "Mister" to avoid military rank interplay. He took copious notes, recording the personal identifying data of the female admin clerks, Bull Conner, Chief Bichet, and Melissa Taylor. He quizzed Frenchie politely but directly on what he saw, what he heard, and what Conner said to him in person. The lengthy interview was conducted professionally, dispassionately, and with no feedback from the agent and no sign of any follow-up needed unless more clarification became necessary. The questions the agent asked rang formulaic. He had been through this drill many times. Leaving, he closed the door to Frenchie's office quietly was the calm before the tempest, the shit storm Chief Bechet accurately forecast. Little did Frenchie anticipate how strongly that dirty storm would blow.

Three days later, the maintenance chief, the full colonel, entered Frenchie's open door and plopped a sheaf of papers on the worn, gray desk.

"Thibodeau, your orders came in."

For the second time in less than two months, new assignment orders appeared unexpectedly out of the blue or the Pentagon. Air Force personnel can expect reassignment roughly every two to four years, not two to four months.

"You're going to the Alaskan Air Command, to be the facilities officer at Shemya. Have fun."

The Colonel turned around and marched off along the corridor, uttering no further words. Shemya Air Force Station lies on the extreme western end of the Alaskan Aleutian Islands, 1500 miles from Anchorage, much closer to Russia than to the US mainland. The base serves as an emergency landing field for aircraft transiting the north Pacific Ocean and as a sometimes refueling stop. It is famous throughout the Air Force for rotten weather and alcoholism. There, addiction is promoted by isolation and boredom accentuated by never-ending wind, overcast skies, and bitter, wet cold. Frenchie read and re-read the assignment orders, stared at the ceiling for a few minutes, then chucked the loose pile into his gray steel wastebasket with a resounding thud. The office door slammed behind him as he left.

***

Soon-to-be-civilian Captain Marcel Thibodeau used his still-valid flight line security pass to access the busy aircraft parking ramp at Luke Air Force Base. His resignation from the United States Air Force proceeded smoothly with no bureaucratic snags. Obviously, the personnel office had been urged to process his paperwork expeditiously. Someone tipped off the clerks to expect his submission, and they were prepared. They knew he wanted to resign his officer's commission and to leave the service quietly and quickly. Once a civilian, the authorities could not easily call him back unwilling to testify, the hidden motivation which greased the exit skids. It did not take much imagination to discern who pulled the strings or why. His status in the U. S. Air Force and his pay would time out when he used his remaining days of leave of absence, a terminal paid vacation. Until then, Frenchie would enjoy his position as a full member of the armed services, but with no duties and no assignments.

F-16s crowded the concrete tarmac, lined up militarily row by row, their gray noses all pointed in the same direction. The airplanes were parked under overhead sun shades. The shades, a kind of carport for fighter planes, shielded the aircraft and their mechanics from the merciless Arizona desert sun.

Frenchie selected a jet not being serviced or repaired. No one hovered around attending to its mechanical needs. Walking slowing around the silent fighter, he looked long and hard at its sleek lines. He took in the sweep-back of its vestigial wings, the thrusting nose, the bubble canopy over the gaping maw of the engine's air intake like a cobra's, not a viper's, hood. To get a better view, he stepped back and looked up to the little metal bird's upright tail, an aerodynamic feature possessed by no actual living bird, much less a falcon.

He peered into the blackened tailpipe, the source of earsplitting noise and fearsome jet thrust. Slowly putting his hand on the fuselage, he stared up toward the unoccupied cockpit, its gold-tinged canopy shut, locked tight, barring unauthorized entry. The aluminum skin was still and lifeless. When the Fighting Falcon prepared for flight, the gray skin would hum with the engine's vibration. Now it was inert, sleeping. Frenchie patted the jet on its nose cone as one fondles a faithful dog, once, twice, and then let his fingers trail along the jet's tapered side. He turned. Spinning on a booted heel, he walked away from the parked F-16, not looking over his shoulder with teary eyes. It was the end of a chapter in his life.

Resignation from the U. S. Air Force had not been an easy thing to do, not an easy choice to make, but one he felt he had to follow through with. The howling bureaucratic winds of the shit storm forecast by the old Creole Chief Master Sergeant had blown away his career or at least his career as a fighter pilot. Yes, he could have endured a series of boring assignments and functionary jobs at a variety of desks, until eligible for retirement, but that is not what he signed up for. Frenchie made his choice, blew the whistle on Bull Conner and was now paying the price.

The Corvette rumbled along Litchfield Road, the major thoroughfare leading south from Luke Air Force Base to I-10. The interstate highway runs east from Jacksonville, Florida across America to Santa Monica, California. At the wide cloverleaf interchange where the air base road meets I-10, Frenchie pulled over to the roadside and stopped the car, silencing the engine. Up ahead, a bright green overhead traffic sign presented two choices; east-bound or west-bound I-10.

Far to the east lay Louisiana. Misty, familiar scenes awaited him there, emitting a golden aura of past good times. The Gulf Coast slacker lifestyle offered him the many pleasures of laid-back Cajun country; gumbo and jambalaya, Cajun music, and *fais-doe-doe* dance parties. Family and friends, bass fishing, and beer drinking waited for him there. Bayou swamp land held warm memories, memories of when times shown golden with Yvette. Memories of passionate sex, heady romance, and the endless possibilities of newlyweds, all now abandoned and cold.

Also waiting back in Cajun country were people he cared about who would want to be told what happened between him and Yvette. His family and hers, scattered along the shores of Bayou Teche, would have questions he did not want to answer. Questions to which he did not know the answers lurked like metaphorical alligators in the dark swamp water of shame, the shame for a failed marriage in devout Catholic culture.

To the west and closer lay California, where generations of Americans have sought alternative lives, new beginnings, fresh starts. He could be anyone he wanted to be in the Golden State. Instead of poling a pirogue down the bayou, he could hang ten from a surfboard in Malibu. Instead of using airplanes to kill people, he could get a proper job, maybe one where his customers would appreciate his efforts and not die. Any other profession would not, could not, offer the satisfaction of flying fighter planes, but what gig does.

Frenchie fired up the car, the engine clearing its throat with a muffled mutter. He snicked the stick shift into first gear and slowly turned right, toward the setting sun, the Pacific Ocean, and beckoning California. I-10 stretched ahead in an unwavering straight line to the Arizona border. The Corvette sped up deliberately, merging with west-bound traffic, then keeping pace with the convoy of lumbering trucks clogging the slow lane. After five minutes, Frenchie shifted down a gear, matted the accelerator pedal, and swerved left into the fast lane. The unleashed sports car leaped ahead, devouring the distance at extra-legal speed, its long hood pointed toward the far horizon and hopefully a fresh life.

Later, at sundown, Frenchie pulled off the highway and stopped on a low bluff overlooking the Colorado River, the swift-flowing waterway dividing Arizona from California. Behind him lay the Sonoran Desert peopled with saguaro cacti, their arms held high in worship to the cloudless sky. Ahead, across the river, the landscape changed instantly to one of desolation and emptiness, as if the flora and fauna recognized the riverine political boundary. This empty-quarter wasteland stretched to the ocean and the fabled City of Los Angeles. It is California's version of Oz. Frenchie did not take the appearance of the desolate, sun-blasted California desert to be a positive omen.

Standing beside his car and looking westward, Frenchie's phone alerted him to two incoming texts. Neither came from Mousse. The messages were the same, sent simultaneously. He recognized both senders' names—the harassed female clerks in Bull Conner's office, LaTonya Jefferson and Miranda Lopez.

The first message read, "Lt. Col Conner was relieved of command and ordered to report to personnel headquarters. We are free, free at last." The second text said, "THANKS, SIR" the only words on the screen, in all caps. He smiled, re-read both messages and sent return texts consisting of only a smiling emoji. Frenchie returned to the car after one last look at the ever-flowing river and drove west.

CHAPTER 18
VANDENBERG SPACE FORCE BASE, LOMPOC, CALIFORNIA

Vandenberg Space Force Base on California's Central Coast, located halfway between Los Angeles and San Francisco, is an eerie, haunted place. It is comprised of wind-swept wasteland and shallow hills scattered with scrubby bushes and stunted trees. Part of the U. S. Air Force Space Command, the base possesses no aircraft. No missions are flown from it. Missing is the frequent roar of jet engines and the sight of fighters, transports, and training planes overhead, as experienced on most air bases. Only the "Scree! Scree!" of red-tailed hawks echo across its empty skies.

These soaring raptors patrol over isolated ranks of eucalyptus trees marching line abreast to the horizon. On most days, the only aviation committed on base is the darting flight of seabirds and the hawks' wheeling orbits overhead. Hawk's cries are popularly perceived in the visual media as the screams of defiance uttered by eagles.

An eagle's natural verbalization is a series of clicks and grunts, not very impressive, or patriotic. So, the red-tailed hawk's more expressive language is dubbed in during editing.

The base stretches for 25 miles along a deserted shoreline dotted with remote beaches crashed by bone-chilling surf. Waves march across the Pacific Ocean, gathering momentum and losing heat until they collide with North America. Very occasional rocket launches generate the only visible and audible indications any activity occupies the time of the few military personnel stationed there. Frenchie felt this lonely, isolated outpost might be ideal to aid his mental transition from *uber*-aggressive airborne warrior to mild-mannered civilian. Vandenberg and the "Space Coast" are well-suited for an ex-pilot quitting flying cold turkey and for one trying to escape more than memories than of lost aviation.

He endured hours of stop-and-go traffic transitioning the overcrowded Los Angeles basin. His Corvette was constrained, trapped in La-La Land's car-choked freeways. North of Santa Barbara, US Highway 101 opened, running free and straight along a spectacular coastline. Then the road turned eastward toward Vandenberg's guarded inland entry gate. After checking into the temporary Bachelor Officer's Quarters, he stopped by the base convenience store. There he bought a bottle of Tennessee sour mash whiskey, a bag of Redi-Pop popcorn, a flask of Tabasco sauce, and a bag of ice. The iconic square liquor bottle with the black label came equipped with a cube-shaped, monogrammed shot glass—a pleasant touch. Frenchie sat drinking on his room's tiny balcony overlooking an air base with no airplanes and no pilots. He had to decide what to do with the next phase of his life.

Douse some popcorn with Tabasco sauce. Munch until the fire gets unbearable. Extinguish the burn with Jack Daniel's on the rocks. Repeat. Think about the future, not the past. Frenchie continued the routine as night crept across the air base's expanse. A job would be nice, keep him occupied for the time being. Preferably an interesting job, one not involving aviation, too many memories there. But where to start? Local area is quiet, laid-back. Just the locale to get his head back together. Normally, he would watch a classic movie on his laptop. Not tonight. Must get some sleep.

As he dozed off, the residual fire in his throat, kindled by fermented red peppers and vinegar aged in used Bourbon barrels, faded. The physical pain was replaced by a conflagration of another sort, another aviation memory, one he could not escape, even when aided by excellent whiskey. In his mind's eye, he saw a MiG-29's burning wreckage tumbling end-over-end to the Strait of Hormuz far below. In the wrecked cockpit slumped the corpse of what, only seconds ago, had been a human being.

***

A handmade sign on the gravel road leading up to the winery read, "Now Hiring. Tasting Room." Frenchie pulled the scrawled cardboard placard off the wooden fence post with a firm tug. Up the slight hill to the Spanish-style building, he followed arrows labeled "Tasting Room." He asked himself, parking the car, "What the hell is a tasting room?"

East of Vandenberg AFB lie the Santa Rita Hills, a gentle land of rolling terrain bifurcated by the Santa Ynez River delta. The gravel stream bed, dry most of the year, stretches a quarter-mile wide as it reaches the cold Pacific Ocean. This geographic feature flowing through a wrinkle, a gap, in the hills allows cool sea air driven by nighttime onshore winds to penetrate inland toward the valleys baking daily in the California sun. A combination of warm days and chilly nights is ideal for the cultivation of specific types of wine grapes. Burgundian varieties such as red Pinot Noir and white Chardonnay thrive on the gentle slopes, spreading in rows across flat, fertile valley floors. Vines caressed in the morning by dense radiation fog and warmed by our nearby star during the afternoon develop complex flavor profiles rivaling those of grapes in legendary Burgundy, France. All at a fraction of the price demanded in Europe.

Santa Rita Hills wineries are small, boutique affairs operated by owner/farmer/vintners. These folk share a passion for top quality wine and a toleration of the precarious finances produced by vinous obscurity. The region remains undiscovered in the global world of fine wine.

The big man behind the rustic wooden bar looked out-of-place indoors. Sun-burnt and rugged, with piercing eyes and rough hands. He obviously longed to be on a tractor in a vineyard or turning grape juice into wine in the winery. His preferred domain was not in a point-of-sale tasting room pouring free samples for raucous bachelorette parties from Southern California.

The movie *Sideways* turned on the plague of partiers who learned under the guise of sampling wine, they could have an ocean of cheap drinks in wineries' tasting rooms.

The raucous groups of free-loaders tended to descend like well-dressed carrion crows on the well-known wine regions such as Napa, Paso Robles, and Sonoma. But their presence was not unknown in the Santa Rita Hills.

"Here alone for some wine tasting?" the bear-sized man asked.

"No, I'm Marcel Thibodeau, Frenchie to my friends, and I'm here for a job," Frenchie replied. He handed the winemaker the torn "Now Hiring" sign.

"What do you know about wine?" the winemaker asked.

"It comes in two flavors; red and white, although white wine looks clear to me."

"What about rosé?"

"That's a mixture of red and white. Right?"

"Uh, not exactly. Have you ever worked in a tasting room?"

The direct question came right up front. The winemaker minced no words. Fielding the inquiry, Frenchie searched his memory banks for some work history, any job that might have a relationship to the employment opportunity on offer.

"I tended bar in my uncle's honky-tonk in New Orleans, Louisiana, the Dew Drop Inn," Frenchie answered.

"Close enough, you're hired. I'm desperate for help," the big man smiled. "For your information, we have no honky-tonks in the Santa Rita Hills, only wineries and brew pubs. No juke boxes, no Cajun bands and no dances."

"I guess progress comes slow to the bayou country," Frenchie said.

"Here's the deal. You pour samples of my wine for visitors, which you then convert into customers.

Describe what makes it special, sell a few bottles, and urge people to join my wine club. You wash the glasses, clean up, and you sweep out at night. Can you handle it?" the winemaker asked.

"I guess I'll have to since I'm already hired."

Over the rest of the morning, Frenchie and the winemaker sounded each other out. The Santa Rita Hills are ideal for grape growing, but they are underpopulated. To staff sales and tasting rooms is a major business challenge. The winemaker, Steve, asked questions concerning Frenchie's background, status, work ethic, and his willingness to learn quickly a new skill set. The two men got along well, interrupted by customers arriving to taste and to purchase wine. Lunchtime, Steve reached under the wooden bar and handed Frenchie two books; a loose-leaf notebook of tasting notes on the winery's recent releases of red, white, and rosé along with a thick, yellow, full-sized paperback, *Wine for Dummies*.

"Commit these to memory, you start at 1000 in the morning," he said.

"I'll need a place to stay when my Air Force time expires and I'm booted off base. Any leads on a room to rent?"

"There's an old travel trailer out back, past the crush pad. You can bunk down there. The only rules are; no smoking, no drugs, and no ugly women."

Later that night, during a break from his frantic cramming, learning the world of wine, Frenchie stepped out on his balcony and looked up at a star-studded sky. Out beyond the neon glow of sprawling California cities, the stars shine, genuine stars, not the phony cinematic variety. Not intense as seen from the cockpit of an F-16, but still a brilliant blue-white. The Milky Way drew his gaze for a minute, then two. Before returning to his studies, Frenchie texted his new job title, Wine Tasting Room Manager, and tentative address to Major Melissa Taylor with little expectation of a reply.

He had but a few days to settle in to a new way of life, new status as a civilian, and to make new friends. One was obvious. Steve, in their brief morning's discussion, seemed to be an intelligent and inciteful man if a bit rough-hewn. The sensitivity required to tease out the subtle taste differences in wine, particularly new, raw wine, carried over to his interpersonal relations. He has sized up Frenchie and said he liked what he saw. Another friend awaited, this one entirely unexpected.

CHAPTER 19
JALAMA BEACH, LOMPOC, CALIFORNIA

She never saw the wind turbine blade coming. The peregrine's vision, using her narrow field-of-view, high-precision region of her retina, had locked onto her intended prey, an immature tern flying just over the surface. Fast in her dive, she cared only for her intercept aim point. She ignored all other inputs. This condition, referred to in fighter pilots' domain as "target fixation," is a potentially fatal mental obsession. The slowly sweeping windmills did not register as a mortal threat, at least not one she recognized. She knew all about other raptors. She knew about eagles who would steal her meal, about crows, usually up to no good. She knew about solid mother earth whose embrace she must avoid at 125 miles an hour. Windmills, new to the Central Coast and present on Earth for only a tiny fraction of a peregrine's evolutionary memory, did not figure into her risk/reward equation in the slightest.

The impact struck her with the blade's midpoint where the rotational speed was not the greatest, saving her life. She endured a fierce shock when her feathered body wrapped itself around the airfoil-shaped surface. A sharp internal crack signaled a broken wing bone accompanied by a flash of intense pain. With her one good wing, she fought her way off the blade and fell out of control in a burst of shattered feathers. Tumbling over the lip of the bluff mounting the windmill, she screamed all the way to the beach below. Uncoordinated flapping and ruffled feathers slowed her fall enough to avoid additional damage on impact with the beach. She hit the soft sand surface with a dull thump and lay there until her mind cleared sufficiently for her to struggle. She tried to get her crippled wing to stroke in concert with her sound one despite the resulting agony. After a few minutes of unproductive flapping and thrashing, she lay still, exhausted and in intense pain. Without hope, the female falcon waited for the darkness to come for her.

Frenchie had gone for an early morning run on the deserted public beach. This dawn was one of his last days as a service member before his resignation became final. Early in the foggy mist, with only the seabirds' cries and the surf's murmur for a soundtrack, he longed to clear his head for the day ahead. Alone on the beach, no one distracted him. He needed to digest mentally the wine lore he crammed into his skull. The wind turbines' whine on the bluff overlook was dissipated, torn into inaudible shreds by the onshore sea breeze. The windmills became familiar on his dawn runs and were unnoticed by him, visual wallpaper in the lonely sea-land environment.

Something caught his eye, a slight movement on the debris-strewn sand between him and the base of the bluff. He was used to seeing small birds hunting for sea scraps and bugs among the heaped mounds of dead kelp strands, but this action seemed different. Fighter pilots are trained to spot an object's transit against a fixed background. Relative motion is their primary means of spotting an approaching airborne threat. That skill can mean the difference between life and death for a pilot, or in this case, a peregrine falcon.

Frenchie stopped and turned toward the unknown creature on the littered beach. Before him, against a shoal of dead kelp, half-stood, half-lay a bird. It was larger than a crow, with a gray-buff back and a mottled, barred white chest. Now still, the bird watched him approach with wide-open eyes, one wing dangling uselessly, its yellow feet buried in the soft sand. Not a gull or a wading shorebird, the wounded creature was obviously a predator. The binocular vision and the hooked beak with its pointed, notched tip shouted the bird's mission in life.

"What's the matter, Buddy? Did you hurt your wing?" Frenchie asked, not expecting a reply.

No answer came from the bird. It continued to fix its unblinking eyes on the approaching human, without expression, seemingly without fear. When he got within six feet, the raptor dipped its head almost imperceptibly, the cruel beak dipping maybe half an inch. Submission, a cry for aid, or something more? It was impossible to tell. Frenchie's heart melted.

"Let's see if we can get you fixed up," Frenchie said.

He took off his windbreaker jacket with the U. S. Air Force logo and threw it over the bird, preparing to pick it up. He hoped the tough, rip-stop cloth would protect him from that bird-killing beak. Under the coat, suddenly in the dark, the bird remained still. Frenchie gathered the jacket folds around the bird and lifted it a few inches. He saw strong, yellow feet tipped with black talons emerge from the loose sand. He relaxed his grip on the bird. Wanting nothing to do with those razor-sharp talons, he pulled the drawstring from his running shorts and tied the bird's feet together. Instinctive or not, he served himself well. To defend themselves, Peregrines fight with their talons. Their beaks are meant only for dispatching prey and dismembering carcasses. Beaks are too near vital eyes to serve as weapons. Once enclosed by enveloping cloth, and in the black, the crippled bird stayed still, as most birds will. Motionless despite the pain generated by the broken wing, she waited. Cradling his captive with both hands, Frenchie started back toward the air base and help.

***

Wrapped in the jacket, the crippled bird remained motionless. Darkness came for her, but not the life-ending blackness she expected. Day-hunting falcons are soothed by the night and comforted by its blackness. When the human approached, she did not know what to expect. She had seen many of their kind from on high. They appeared to her to be strange but uninteresting creatures, neither prey nor threat and thus not worthy of extended consideration. The man towered over her, but his body language told the bird he did not intend to kill her. A slight head nod acknowledged the message. Even racked by pain waves, she realized this man represented her only hope. She waited for what was to come in the comforting folds of the United States Air Force windbreaker. Her life was now in the human's hands, literally.

CHAPTER 20
VANDENBERG SPACE FORCE BASE, LOMPOC, CALIFORNIA

The major was an officer in the US Army's Veterinary Corps, a unit established over a century ago to minister to the needs of cavalry horses. Slender and bespectacled, he showed the world a caring face, one which looked on animals kindly. Army vets take care of all the armed services' working dogs. These are the canines who look for drugs and Bad Guys, who stand guard duty, and dogs who conduct search and rescue operations. In their spare time, the army's dedicated animal doctors treat pets and companion animals of active duty personnel on a *pro bono* basis. He looked up from his desk when Frenchie carried a sloppily wrapped bundle into the veterinary office on Vandenberg Space Force Base.

"Doc, I'm Captain Thibodeau and I have a challenge for you," Frenchie said.

"Put him on the table here. What's the problem?" the vet replied.

As the vet separated Frenchie's tangled windbreaker from its contents, the first feature to emerge was two sets of black, razor-sharp talons, bound with cotton string. The startled doc took a quick step backward and starred at the still hidden animal lying on the stainless steel exam table. Frenchie carefully completed the slow unveiling, holding the bird still. A long, low whistle streamed from the vet's surprised face as the bird emerged from the crumpled jacket. Her eyes, always wide open, blinked under the bright lights in the clinic's overhead. Her head darted from side to side, taking in the bizarre environment she found herself in. Still, no struggling from her, being held motionless by Frenchie with soft hands.

"Captain, what do you know about birds?" the doc asked.

"My mother and my grandmother raised chickens."

"This is not a chicken. What you've brought me here is a peregrine falcon, a female judging by her size. Where did you get her and why?"

"I saw her struggling beneath a windmill near the beach. I think she has a broken wing and I think you can and should fix her. She needs to fly again."

With Frenchie cradling the bird, the vet, carefully avoiding the bound talons and hooked beak, extended her wings each in turn and quickly diagnosed which bone was indeed broken.

The raptor lay motionless in Frenchie's hands, her unblinking eyes fixated on him, ignoring the vet's cautious movements. She quivered in pain when he reached the point of injury, but without thrashing. It was as if she understood her last chance for flight depended on these strange humans hovering over her.

"I think I can fix her wing. It isn't badly splintered, it's what we call a green-stick fracture. If we keep it immobilized, the bone will probably heal in time. While I work on her, you need to go to the commissary and buy a package of beef stew meat. A bird this size needs to eat at least twice a day and she's strictly a carnivore."

"Falcons eat cows. Who knew?" Frenchie said.

"She prefers raw red meat. Our commissary doesn't sell fresh-killed pigeon. Once we get her stabilized, we'll need to get her to the raptor rescue people in Ojai. That's south of Santa Barbara. They'll know how to get her back into the air."

Leaving the vet to his work, Frenchie drove to the commissary, the food market on the base, and bought a pre-packed tray of beef stew meat pre-cut into one-inch cubes. Then he stopped by the base exchange and purchased the largest dog crate which fit into a Corvette's passenger seat and a dog's water bowl.

Back at the clinic, the vet had set and bound the bird's left wing and put her in an empty cat cage. Peering out from behind the mesh bars, she continued to focus on only one of the two humans hovering over her, Frenchie. He put two red meat cubes on the cage floor in front of her and stepped back, closing the cage slowly. The peregrine starred at Frenchie, then shuffled over to the meat, her legs at last unbound. Holding a piece of blood-dripping beef in one talon, she ravenously tore into the flesh, downing it in two bites. The second morsel followed in short order. The bird looked up from the cage, keeping her gaze fixed on Frenchie. He thought he saw a slight nod of the feathered head, but maybe that is just what he wanted to see.

"Can I keep her, doc?"

"Certainly not. Peregrines are an endangered species. You must be licensed by the federal government and the state to keep one. If they catch you trying to make one into a pet, they'll put you under the jail. Besides, as I said, this is not a chicken. She requires the care and training of skilled falconers until they can release her back into the wild."

The vet looked hard and long at Frenchie, whose attention never left the bird while she ate. He shrugged his shoulders and turned to leave.

"I have to go out to the missile launch pads to check on some dog kennels. When I get back, I want this bird gone. I will assume you have taken her to the Ojai Raptor Center. Here's a card with their address. Got that, Captain?" the vet said.

"Yes sir," said Frenchie, soon to be a civilian.

"Good, lock the door behind you when you leave and good luck."

***

Later that afternoon, after closing the tasting room for the day, Frenchie stood on the winery's concrete crush pad. It was a tennis court-sized flat slab where bins of grapes are converted into the grape juice destined to be wine. Crushed not by uncouth peasants' bare feet but by a mechanical de-stemmer/crusher from France.

The sky above to the west shown with an amber light, heralding the approaching sunset. In far distant regions to the north a low rumble, like the muttering of an unseen but powerful god, echoed across the Santa Rita hills. In a way, the rumble did represent a god, the seductive, winsome deity of flight. Frenchie worshiped her for years, obeyed her commands, served her rituals, and made the sacrifices she demanded. His reward for unquestioned loyalty had been the opportunity to do something only a tiny fraction of humanity could boast of — flying jet fighters. Now, he turned his back on her, rejected her charms. To follow his ethical sense, to right a grave wrong, he set in motion a series of events resulting in his ejection, symbolic not actual, from the fighter pilot priesthood.

Looking north, he heard not the throaty roar of F-16s but the high-pitched howl of F-18 Hornet fighter aircraft from Lemoore Naval Air Station. Their soprano thunder rolled across the coastal skies. The noise disturbed the customary silence blanketing Vandenberg and the nearby vineyards. A formation of US Navy fighter jocks was getting in practice flights before dark. Frenchie mentally followed the sound. The maneuvering aircraft were too distant to see. He listened to their sirens' screams until the din died and the sun silently set.

Frenchie's grand passion he had deserted for the chance for another love. Gone was the thin-lipped bitch of aviation, forever jealous, for the allure of a real woman whose lips he remembered for their hungry, sensual softness. She was a flesh-and-blood woman who never responded to his many attempts at communication. However, even if Frenchie's jet flying days were over, another of his friends had the chance to return to the skies, with his help.

He entered the run-down travel trailer's flimsy door making sure it securely shut behind him and fetched two pieces of red meat from the tiny fridge. In a corner of the trailer a peregrine falcon, a female, sat quietly on a makeshift perch. She accepted the food offering and began tearing one of the morsels apart while her gaze never left Frenchie. Watching closely, he reached for the other beef cube, moving slowly to not alarm the bird. He ate the raw meat, chewing the fat-laced bite, blood dripping from his chin, the taste of raw steak filling his mouth. The peregrine watched him intently.

Chapter 21
Nowhere, West Texas

Abilene, Texas receded in the rear-view mirror, its flat topography shrunk by the rearward flow of Interstate 10. The city slowly faded into the dusty horizon, leaving nothing but a smudge far to the east, behind the car, lost in shimmering heat waves radiated by baking asphalt. West Texas is a land whose beauty lies underground, not on the surface. Oil wells, drilling derricks, and storage tanks littered the landscape, reaching far out of sight on the left and right, joined by pipelines. The industrial infrastructure was used to extract and store the black stuff. Pool table terrain dotted by scraggly mesquite trees and shapeless bushes lined the highway, which had not thrown a curve, even a gentle one, in the last three dozen miles.

The engine's drone, the tires' hum, and the slipstream's rush past the locked-up convertible top proved oddly comforting; an automotive white noise machine. Still, Mousse gripped the steering wheel with clenched hands. She could have lashed the wheel, pointed it straight ahead. Only random truck-generated wind vortexes produced the need for path corrections. Not until she passed Big Spring, Texas 100 miles west of

Abilene, did she think to relax. The car's radio played a local station, proudly claiming every song on the air featured Texas in some way. *San Antonio Rose*, by Bob Wills and his Texas Playboys, proved to be her last audio straw. She switched the aural wallpaper to satellite radio, to a smooth jazz station. San Antonio did not hold recent fond memories for Melissa Taylor, late of the United States Air Force.

She had been poked, prodded, tested, and interrogated by the aviation medicine center staff. Each series of tests led to others. The evaluations and interviews confirmed the preliminary diagnosis of PTSD made downrange. But no one at the hospital seemed to know exactly what stress caused the syndrome. Conversation with a shrink might reveal the problem. An appointment with an overworked psychologist made Mousse's schedule. The head doc canceled the session when the OSI investigation blew everything up. The stress fountain welled up from an event that was the subject of a possible criminal case. Doctor/client confidentiality is waived when there is probable cause of a suspected crime. The shrink refused to take part unless any confidences expressed by Melissa could be kept just that, in confidence. The U. S. Air Force bureaucracy said no.

The investigation quickly devolved into a "she said, he said" standoff. Bull Conner claimed Captain Taylor offered him sex in return for an outstanding performance report, which he was only too happy to provide. Her claims of coercion and harassment seemed to carry equal weight with the Judge Advocate General's Office. The JAG is the organization of military lawyers charged with trying any suspected crime. Command authorities at the base in San Antonio just wanted the whole mess to go away. A judgement that the sorry situation was merely a case of "boys will be boys" and "girls will be girls" when isolated in a foreign land was compiled. It was not released by the JAG. Conventional wisdom at the Officer's Club bar said the JAG, because of too much adverse publicity in the press, was under command pressure to suppress the number of sexual harassment cases. They were told to sweep as many as possible under a legal rug. Many suspected the wing commander in Saudi Arabia, under whose oversight the events occurred, also weighed in with a thumb on the scales of justice, trying to keep his own record clean.

Mousse's promotion was placed on hold, probably forever. Then, the two enlisted admin clerks in Conner's office, Jefferson and Miranda, came forward, accompanied with, and supported by, Chief Bichet. After their testimony, Conner's M.O. became clear, but the die had been cast and officialdom never likes to reverse course unless shamed into doing so by an outside organization such as the civilian media. Instead of being tried in a court martial proceeding, Lieutenant Colonel Conner was allowed to quietly leave the U. S. Air Force with a General Discharge. Captain Melissa A. Taylor was allowed to stay in limbo. Chief Bichet retired, returned home to New Orleans, and slept soundly.

With her official reputation in tatters and her military career prospects dim, Mousse decided to cash in her U. S. Air Force chips. With a questionable episode and a cancelled promotion marring her record in the highly competitive race to command a squadron, she would probably never achieve her long-held goal of leadership. Digging deeper, she realized the golden glow of her immediate prize, major's leaves, had been tarnished by the dirty fingerprints she left when she reached for them. Another flying assignment was also unlikely. Few existing squadron commanders would risk a woman pilot with her record.

Driving on, she asked herself, *when did my life-time goal become an obsession? How did that obsession corrupt my personal morals and leave me vulnerable to Conner's pressure? Why didn't I go to the OSI when this all started?* After this colossal screw-up, a fresh start in life beckoned. She left military service, not with a bang, but a whimper.

Her first stop as a civilian was her parents' home in Abilene, to decompress for a few days. Now that too was lost in the mirror. Why did she feel the need to travel west, to California? The Golden State's allure of a land where a person might re-invent herself was part of it. California has always sung a sweet siren song of fresh starts. Is that a valid dream? There was but one way to find out if California is truly the anti-Texas.

Her father went on record opposed to her migration. He held the opinion California might be contagious. Stay too long on the Left Coast and she might ditch her Porsche for a Prius and vote Libertarian. However, once in California, *You can check out anytime you like, but you can never leave.* Proud of his patriotic, fighter pilot daughter, he was not so sure she would succeed out of uniform.

Her mother, true to type, also wanted Melissa to stay home. Her words echoed in Mousse's head as she headed west.

"That nice young man down at the hardware store, I think he's the manager, asked about you last week. You went to high school with him, why don't you stop in and say hello?"

Melissa was not willing to trade the rigid U.S. Air Force social structure for the equally stifling West Texas culture, however well-intentioned her parents. Life there involved blue jeans, big belt buckles, pickup trucks, cowboy hats, and little else. Conformation to the norm was strongly but pleasantly enforced. How are you going to keep them down on the farm after they have seen Paris, France, as well as Paris, Texas?

Her stay with her parents, in the house she called home, helped to sooth her psyche. Only one shower a day proved to be adequate and she could finally look in a mirror. The PTSD symptoms, noticed by her family, diminished but by no means left her entirely. In Melissa's family, psychological ailments were not a matter for discussion. Any such problems were meant to be taken care of by oneself.

She carefully folded her formal uniforms and her flight suits, stacked her awards and decorations plaques, and placed photos of her standing next to an F-16 on top. The lot was stashed in dresser drawers in her childhood room. She gently closed to door to her bedroom, kissed her parents, and drove west.

She had stopped answering Frenchie's texts and emails, not feeling worthy enough to do so. The whole sorry saga of the OSI investigation did not recommend itself to be told to an ex, and maybe future, lover. Frenchie did not understand what she had gone through to be promoted. She had warned him to disengage. Still, he kept updating her regularly on his status and location. Those gestures, attempts at communication, meant something to her. Being honest with herself, digging deep again, she understood her choice of destination was driven in part by the urge to see Frenchie again. Yet, she was not ready to let him know she was coming, uncertain how such a reunion would go. *What does a tasting room manager actually do?* she asked herself. In Texas, tasting rooms are called "saloons."

In two days of hard driving, she could be on California's Central Coast.

Chapter 22
Santa Rita Hills, California

Frenchie's new and unexpected vocation, tasting room manager and super salesperson, while less hazardous than his previous profession, flying the F-16, seemed to suit him. He enjoyed the interaction with the variety of folks visiting the winery. To learn from some of them the wine world's nuances, he asked questions. The answers helped nearly as much as his nightly cramming.

The ex-pilot soon discovered selling wine entailed an entirely different interpersonal skill set than life in a fighter squadron. His service mates, all pilots, female or male, were a highly competitive bunch. They, overtly or subtly, challenged each other on the ground and in the air as a matter of course. Persuasion usually involved a difficult aerial maneuver. Relationships were transactional and often a zero-sum head game.

His two trysts with Mousse in the desert illustrated the transient nature of personal relations in a squadron.

Their coupling untypically benefited both parties equally. Frantically consummating the interaction and intercourse left no time for the intimacy they both craved. Still, he could not get her off his mind. He knew her body, inside and out, but not her inner self, who she was, what she wanted out of life.

Retailing wine in a tasting room was nothing like seducing Mousse, if that was what happened and not vice versa. His ego refused to consider that it was he who had been seduced. It was even less like joshing with the other pilots in the crew room. "You're not expert enough to enjoy this bottle of cabernet sauvignon," never resulted in a sale. Challenge wine tasting was not an effective selling technique.

In air combat, a pilot's first move is critical and may dictate the engagement outcome. Sales presented a similar dynamic. Frenchie learned to follow a prospective customer's lead. After pouring an ounce or two of a sample, he waited for the visitor's visible or verbal reaction.

For the knowledgeable drinker, he stressed the exclusivity of a particular bottle. He pitched the unique *terroir,* the French word for a grape-growing environment, of the surrounding Santa Rita Hills. Details of the wine's production also scored big points, as did comparisons with the products of classic French *chateaux.*

Less knowledgeable visitors required a more original approach. For them, Frenchie talked up various flavor profiles and suggested the food pairings the wine cried out for. Whereas in the USAF, any definitive opinion was immediate grounds for dispute, he never disagreed or argued with prospective customers. The winning tactics involved some version of "A quality wine is what tastes good to you, regardless of its cost or pedigree."

To clinch a wine club membership became his ultimate goal. Enrolled, a member would automatically receive a case shipped to their home four times a year. Winemaker Steve loved the locked-in deliveries of his output. He really dug guaranteed periodic sales.

The Santa Rita Hills are not a "in" destination in the domain of Bacchus, at least not yet. Thus, Frenchie and Steve avoided the typical "how much can we drink for cheap" day-tripping crowd from Los Angeles. Oenophiles dedicated to finding an obscure winery in an off-the-beaten-path wine region tended to be knowledgeable and interested. They were eager to discuss vintages, vines, and flavor profiles. Compared to the Dew Drop Inn in NOLA, there were no abusive drunks to eject, no bar fights to break up, and no underage drinkers. The most interesting thing about the job was he never knew who would walk in the door.

Raven hair, long and straight, flowed down her back reaching toward her narrow waist. Dark, dark eyes flashed, taking in the tasting room scene. She wore a tight, short sweater sans bra, baring her midriff and below, far below. Slacks, low-cut, falling off her hips, were tight enough and thin enough to show off the vertical slit in her lady parts. Stiletto heels, black like the rest of her outfit, finished the image she tried hard to project. Was that alluring or revenge? She stood silently at the bar's far end, not moving, but watching Frenchie ring up purchases for the day's final customers. It was late in the day. He pretended to ignore her with little success. The room was empty at last except for the two, wary of each other. Frenchie turned to the woman across the bar.

"Of all the tasting rooms, in all the wineries, in all the world, she walks into mine. *Bonjour Yvette,*" he said, flashing a quick smile. He poured her a glass of pale-yellow chardonnay. "Try this, it's spectacular."

"I remember when we both enjoyed *Casablanca. Bonjour Marcel, Sa va bien?*"

She had asked, literally, "Are you going well?" using the familiar form, "*va,*" of the French verb *aller* meaning, "to go." The familiar form, second person singular, is used in French to converse with relatives, spouses, and lovers, which are not mutually exclusive categories in Cajun country. However, Cajun argot always employs the familiar form universally, reflecting either the closeness of Cajun personal relations or of their use of sloppy French. It was hard for Frenchie to tell in which mode she meant it. He set a verbal trap to get a better reading.

"*Oui, trés bien. Et vous?, ou et tu ?*" Frenchie replied, using first the much more formal pronoun of address, "*vous.*" This form is used for business dealings, strangers and for lovers whose romantic status needs to stay under cover, if not under the covers. It is also used to speak to ex-lovers. He then added "*ou et tu,*" and you, using the familiar form, giving Yvette the option to accept a subtle offer of familiarity.

Yevette nodded in thanks for the offered glass and perhaps also in recognition the message "*tu*" conveyed. As she silently sipped the shining white wine, she pulled her shoulders back ever so slightly stretching her abbreviated sweater even tighter across her unbound breasts, showing them off. Eyes met, then each pair turned away. Yvette sipped the offered chardonnay, waiting for the man she called Marcel, to speak, but silence reigned in the room for long minutes. Setting her now-empty glass on the wooden bar, she slid a stuffed brown paper envelope across the wooden bar to Frenchie.

"Here are the final divorce decree and your check for one-half the proceeds from the house sale after the mortgage was paid off," she said. The Cajun lilt in her speech brightened up the empty room.

After he picked up the package and placed it under the counter, she went on.

"There's not much left. Is there?"

"No, Yvette, there isn't much left of anything, but there could be. Would you like some more wine? Our estate pinot noir is outstanding. Two glasses will set you free."

"I'm not sure I want to be free. How about you?"

"Yvette, why are you here dressed fit to kill? You could have mailed the papers and the check instead of prancing in here looking like the star of a wet dream."

"Thanks for the compliment, I think. I'm staying with a friend in Santa Barbara. I wanted to see for myself if any spark remained left between us. I still don't know."

"And to show me what I'm missing?"

"*Peut-être. Au revoir,* Marcel. *Bonne chance.* (Perhaps. Goodbye Marcel. Good luck)."

She turned to go, striding across the hardwood floor, her hips swinging to the staccato beat of her sky-high heels. Winemaker Steve appeared in the door as she approached it. He held the door open for her as she bounced toward him. Yvette turned back toward Frenchie, her curves now in a back-lit in profile silhouette. She cocked one leg across the other.

"We'll always have Paris, won't we?" she laughed.

"Yes, and the Big Easy. It was easy back then, *N'est pas?* he replied.

Yvette paused, motionless, her cocked leg quivering, deciding which way to turn, for seconds which seemed like hours. At last, she spun on a heel and walked away.

Steve was busy covertly checking out the expanse of smooth bare skin between her short sweater and her slacks, cut far below her flat stomach. He saw the tops of her pelvic joints peeking out. He continued starring as she crossed the parking lot, her butt cheeks rising and falling. Through the open door, Frenchie saw her climb alone into a pickup truck, the same one parked outside their house in Phoenix the night of the epic dust storm. The owner of the truck was nowhere to be seen.

"Who the hell was that? Steve asked.

"My wife, check that, my ex-wife."

"She's your ex! What are you, man, gay?"

"No, just dumb."

Frenchie fell silent, looking downward while he carefully washed the glass she used, setting it back on a top shelf by itself, ready and waiting. Before he could sweep up and leave, Steve poured four glasses with samples of red wine from two unlabeled bottles, "shiners" as naked bottles are called in winery vernacular. He had brought them up from underneath the bar. One Bordeaux-style bottle, one Burgundy-style, made up the pair. Putting a pair of goblets on opposite sides of a tasting room table, Steve motioned Frenchie to take a seat.

"Frenchie, let's talk. This is zinfandel I'm considering producing in the winery. One is from Santa Ynez, where the climate, the *terroir,* is hot. The other is from here, where it's not. I need your opinion on these and you need mine on some other stuff."

"Sure, Steve. I feel this could be the beginning of a beautiful friendship."

"You've been watching too many old movies. Try both zins and tell me what you think."

Frenchie sipped a taste from each glass, swishing the wine around in his closed mouth, then opening his lips and inhaling over a mouth-pool of zinfandel. Instead of spitting out the samples as per formal winetasting protocol, he swallowed each. It seemed the thing to do after watching Yvette parade once again into and out of his life.

Steve went on, "Since you've been working here, sales in the tasting room have doubled and wine club membership is way up. We're shipping tons of wine, cases and cases. You have a knack for demonstrating and selling wine. I'm jacking up your salary. If this keeps up, I may have to cut you a slice of the action with a commission on sales. What about the zins?"

"The first, in the Bordeaux bottle, is wild and intense, a big, dark drink with a big kick, hard to tame but probably worth it. It's hot, high in alcohol, not complex, easy to understand. The other presents itself as more subtle, refined, smooth, and peppery instead of fruity. It's not in your face like the first. It's less intoxicating up front but with a longer finish, this one would take some thought. For your info, I haven't been binging on old movies, just memorizing *Wine for Dummies*."

"Well done, You've nailed the two zins, Frenchie. Before I forget, today while you were at lunch, some babe came in and asked for you by name here in the tasting room. Didn't give her name, seemed to think you would know her. She stood about five-six, or five-seven with blond hair and slender. Pretty. a real looker, but it was hard to tell. She dressed like a dude in slack jeans and a lumberjack shirt. She had a serious expression on her face."

Frenchie starred at Steve; his eyebrows raised. He poured himself and Steve a generous serving of zinfandel from the second shiner.

"So, you know her, who is she?"

"Maybe I used to, an ex-squadron mate."

Steve swirled the ruby liquid in his wineglass containing the second zin, twirling the goblet by its stem. He cupped his calloused hands under the bowl. The heat from his palms released the zinfandel's aroma, its signature bouquet. He inhaled the vapor and held it in, to better understand what he had before him.

"Frenchie, there was something deep in this woman of mystery, something I noticed. It wasn't obvious, but was there."

Steve inhaled a nose-filling breath of vapor from the mouth of his glass, his eyes closed in contemplation. Frenchie had discovered that Steve thought deeper when he was tasting and judging wine. Evidently the mental effort required to discern subtle aroma nuances spilled over into the world of personal communication. He continued.

"She had a look in her eyes, a distinctive look, one I'm not familiar with. I've only seen it in two other places. Frenchie, you have the look from time to time when you're closing a sale. The other example is the bird you keep in my old trailer. I've seen you take walks after work with it perched on your arm. That bird has the same look as you do and the visitor flashed. When I see it, my blood runs cold."

"She's a peregrine falcon," Frenchie said, downing another swig of the subtle zin.

"Yikes! There's like 10 in the entire state and you've got one here. You understand they're a protected species, don't you?"

"Actually, they're making a comeback. There's a breeding pair nesting on the rock up in Morro Bay. In between my wine education, I've been researching peregrines and falconry."

Steve continued after a long, deep drink of zinfandel. He looked across to Frenchie, putting his glass down and gripping the table with both hands.

"If they catch us with that bird, California State Fish and Wildlife or the Feds will give me life without parole. You, they'll hang. I should kick the both of you off the property, but I can't. You're doing too good a job for me. What do you intend to do with this chicken hawk?"

"She has a broken wing. I will get her back in the air, then release her into the wild. In the meantime, she can scare the birds away from your grapes. Put her on the payroll as temporary help."

Steve leaned back, his chair squeaking, and looked up at the ceiling, then at Frenchie.

"OK," he said. "Oh, one other thing, the mystery babe with the killer stare left something for you."

The winemaker took a business card out of his work shirt pocket and placed it, face down, on the oak table. He slid it across to Frenchie like a hole card, which it could be. Frenchie picked the card up with both hands and read it.

"Where's the Ragged Point Inn and Resort?" he asked Steve.

"Would you believe it's on Ragged Point, north up Highway 1. It's on the south end of Big Sur, two-hours by Corvette. We're closed tomorrow. Take your bird with you in case you don't come back."

CHAPTER 23
SANTA RITA HILLS, CALIFORNIA

Day by day, the throbbing pain in her left wing slowly subsided. Bit by bit, she could extend both wings evenly and hold them out with only minor discomfort. Their sky-ready outline cast shadows on her cage's floor. Not restless while well-fed on raw beef cubes and shredded chicken, she endured captivity with quiet dignity. An apex predator, the peregrine was comfortable with inactivity between hunting flights and between meals. Instead of perching on a rocky ledge overlooking Morro Bay, she was forced to hunker down, confined in the travel trailer's cage. Through the small windows specked with dirt, she could see rows of grapevines and a tiny slice of blue. Occasionally, a sparrow or a starling flew by, provoking a predatory urge. She spread her wings, stiff with inaction, as if to push off in passionate pursuit, but all in vain.

Predators waste no effort when not hunting or mating. They are inactive, moving only when the hunger muse calls. Vivid images present themselves: a pride of lions dozing on the veld, a wolf pack redolent in the sun, a California cougar sprawled, legs askance, in a scrub oak tree. All are conserving energy for the next killing spree and meal.

The female falcon fit this behavior model with one unique exception. A few times a day, the urge to take flight came over her after the human left the trailer. The call of the open sky was still there, operating in the background like a hidden program, but there all the same. She spread her wings and remembered, dreamed she soared over Morro Rock. In her mind, she wheeled in an aerobatic mating ritual with her mate. She dove into a plunging stoop, and then traded airspeed for altitude, zoomed skyward, stopped in mid-air just in time to alight on her rocky aerie. Daydream over, she carefully folded her wings and waited for the man to return with their evening meal.

Often, when the fare included raw beef, he shared a bite with her, each taking half of the cube. This never happened with raw chicken, which she recognized as some sort of bird kill. She never knew why the human did not enjoy a morsel or two of tasty, very rare chicken.

The peregrine developed a grudging appreciation for the man who both kept her earthbound and who kept her fed. Inter-species affection was not part of the deal. Affection rings as too strong a word, too alien a concept, to apply to a creature whose life is normally sustained by inter-species destruction. The man brought the food. He cleaned her mews, the name for a raptor cage. He filled her water bowl and spoke to her. Those actions were enough to generate toleration bordering on underlying respect. Falconers know this. They count on the dynamic to play out whenever a bird is released to fly free and hunt. If the inter-species bond is powerful enough, the bird will come back to its handler and to benign captivity. Raptors raised from eggdom by humans seldom flee. But sometimes, the open sky's lure is too compelling for a bird who has once tasted freedom. The bird departs on its own, free, free at last.

One early evening, he unwrapped a brown paper package as usual. But instead of a meat supply, the parcel contained various items she had never seen. The two jesses came out first, flexible straps of buttery kangaroo leather. He could fasten one end of each jess to a leg and the other to his wrist. Then he put a helmet-like leather cap, a hood, over her head, encasing her in darkness. Not the fearsome final darkness of death, but the comforting darkness of a benevolent night. It calmed her. Finally, he donned a thickly padded rawhide glove, long and resembling a knight's gauntlet. This allowed her to perch on his forearm or grasp his fist with her talons without severing one of his arteries. Thus outfitted, the man and the bird left the trailer together.

Outside, he took off the blinder. She saw the sky's bowl for the first time in what seemed like an eon in bird time. The falcon looked left and right, scanning the horizon for what, crows? eagles? Or maybe a killing wind turbine. She flexed her wings, flapping them methodically. He held tight to the jesses with his cupped fingers, preventing her from leaving his arm.

He strode through the vineyard which surrounded the trailer on three sides, carrying the peregrine on his left arm. The bird periodically stroked her wings in the cool evening air. Seeing the feared predator, a flock of starlings abandoned their assault on the ripening grape clusters and took panicked flight. The swirling black cloud of small birds, called a "murmuration" of starlings, foamed overhead for a few seconds. Then they exited the local airspace looking for a safer field to raid.

Back in the trailer and back in the mews, the man looked at her. She returned his gaze, unblinking.

"Excellent job with the starlings. They'll soon learn you can't fly. But you will. I won't, but you will. I promise."

CHAPTER 24
BIG SUR, CALIFORNIA

North of the Vandenberg space base with its earth-shaking rockets and north of the Santa Rita Hills with their rows of wine grapes marching in formation to the horizon, California's Central Coast flattens out. The land becomes rolling grasslands, verdant and green in the rainy winter, brown and dry in the summer heat. Up the coast, the mounded hills retreat eastward, leaving relatively flat terrain between themselves and the Pacific Ocean. This landscape gap is occupied by cattle ranches trailing off onto deserted and rocky beaches. Towns and people are scarce. Dividing this solitary place is coastal California's main street, the famed Pacific Coast Highway, the PCH, Highway 1.

Outside the tiny town of San Simeon, bands of zebras mingle with the scattered, grazing cows, the only wild zebra herds in the Western Hemisphere. The animals descend from those released from news media mogul William Randolph Hearst's private zoo in the 1930s. On the slopes leading up to Hearst's bespoke castle (Hearst

Castle is more like a sprawling hacienda than a proper Medieval fortification) another non-native species roams free. Also imported and then abandoned by Hearst, Barbary sheep with their curled, long horns clamor over the rocky craigs, frequently lost in low-hanging clouds, moving wraiths in the mist.

The zebras' black and white stripes and the ghostly sheep illustrate the air of unreality haunting this land. It is a scene not of this time and space. The central seacoast is an achingly lonely place, inhospitable to grape vines, sparsely populated, friendly only to creatures with four legs; domestic bovines, alien Moroccan ruminates, and feral African equines. Further north yet, past San Simeon, the hills, now rugged, steep, and densely wooded, reach their rocky fingers for the ocean, displacing the exotic animals. Beaches disappear under salt water where the vertical cliffs tumble into the sea, the sand disappearing like the last vestiges of what passes for normalcy in California to the south.

This unworldly place is called "Big Sur." Few call it home, less than a thousand souls in 100 miles. As the hills advance westward, the previously arrow-straight highway begins to wind and twist, rising and falling with the increasingly rugged terrain. After an asphalt corkscrew of climbing hairpin curves, the PCH scrambles up to Ragged Point. It is the unofficial southern entrance to Big Sur. Perched high on a grassy promontory jutting out into the Pacific Ocean sits the Ragged Point Inn. The tourist stop is a tidy collection of resort hotel rooms, a restaurant/bar, a coffee shop, a gas station, and a hamburger stand. Despite the ordinary commercial attractions, visitors fall under the spell of one of the most breath-taking scenic views on the planet, the Big Sur

ED COBLEIGH

coast. The air/sea landscape shows spectacularly, even when seen through the mail-slot windscreen of a speeding Corvette.

The man removed her leather hood after she perched on a homemade wooden peg in the converted dog crate. With the car's convertible top up, the plastic box barely fit in the right seat. She could see out the windshield and the right-side window as the scenery flowed by, blurred up close, distinct in the distance. Clever creatures, these humans. He made the bird and himself move across the ground without the obvious expenditure of energy. No flapping, no stroking the air, no riding the wind while balancing the forces of lift, drag, and gravity, only effortless movement. That is all she experienced. Together, their speed clocked a relatively moderate 75 miles an hour. It seemed to be readily achieved. Impressive even to a peregrine falcon, a bird not given to easy envy.

***

For obvious security reasons, the desk clerk would not confirm Ms. Melissa Taylor was a guest at the resort. He did not admit to having seen anyone fitting her description, i.e. blonde female fighter pilot. Frenchie left the motel office and walked toward the small park occupying the bluff's extreme westward point overlooking the ocean. Parked outside one low building sat a Porsche sporting a United States Air Force Academy decal on the rear window and Texas plates. It had to be her car.

He found her at the guardrail mounted on the cliff's edge. She stood motionless, looking northward. From Ragged Point on, jagged ridges command the landscape with precipitous slopes falling directly into the relentless surf. The restless ocean foamed and pushed against the bluffs' bases while the tops of the almost-mountains remained lost in a cloudy, wind-driven mist. It was a scene of constant motion versus timeless endurance.

She held the pipe guard rail with both hands, her blond hair, longer now, streaming in the brisk sea breeze. Transfixed by the wild Big Sur coastline, it did not appear she heard him approach. She wore loose-fitting jeans, an extra-long lumberjack shirt hiding her ass, and a dark blue windbreaker, collar flipped up. A U. S. Air Force logo, flaunting stylized silver wings, splayed across her shoulders.

Frenchie sat on a park bench set 20 feet back from and facing the yawning precipice. He raised his voice against the breeze.

"Hi, Mousse. Or should I say, Major Taylor?"

He instantly, but still too late, realized the folly of starting a conversation with a reminder of her promotion and the history of how she obtained it. It was not the smoothest opening move he ever made. Without turning around, she replied over her shoulder; the wind carrying her words, laced with salt air, to him.

"It's Melissa now, just Melissa. I'm not a major and I never will be. Someone informed the OSI about Conner's act and they investigated. Their report got my promotion canceled. I resigned my commission. I'm leaving the Air Force."

Frenchie caught his breath, inhaling through pursed lips, and sat firmly back against the bench's seatback. Not knowing what to say, he said nothing. Melissa pivoted in slow motion and faced him, her narrow waist leaning against the guardrail. Now at her rear, the wind streamed her blonde locks across her face, unnoticed.

"Holy shit, Mousse, or rather, Melissa. That's a serious step. Why?"

"I couldn't live with myself any longer and no one volunteered to live with me," she answered. "I discovered the promotion wasn't worth the price I paid. Then even that too was taken away. My dream turned into a nightmare, not the hallucination you predicted."

Her voice broke on the word "dream" and she experienced trouble finishing the sentence. Frenchie slid over on the bench, motioning to her to join him.

"You can change your job, change your dreams, but you can never change your call sign by yourself. You'll always be "Mousse" to me," he said. "You'll always fly the F-16 in my memory, and rather well."

She hesitated as she walked away from the cliff, then turned and sat on the bench next to him. Melissa crossed her legs in the slow, sensuous way he always found breathtakingly sexy. Silence again reigned, broken only by the wind stirring nearby Monterey pine trees and by the crashing waves breaking far below them.

He reached out tentatively and rested his hand on top of her thigh, feeling her toned leg firm under her loose jeans. She uncrossed her legs. He slipped his fingers between her thighs, halfway up past her knees. It was only the third time he ever touched her, except for an occasional high five, and the first time they touched tenderly. Memories of the frantic encounters in the desert he could not ignore. The images came flooding back in a hot rush of desire. She leaned her head on his shoulder, wind-driven hair covering her face.

"You said no one would live with you. You didn't ask me," he said.

"You can't. I'm damaged goods. Why would you want a prostitute, a whore?

Her voice sounded softer than he ever heard it, yet an icy chill flowed through her words. He did not have to look at her to know that her eyes flashed, cold and hard.

The word "prostitute" cut him like a Bowie knife, deep and quick. The word was the terrible term he taunted her with in the desert. Like a blade thrust, it was not possible to pull it back unbloodied.

"Dammit, Mousse. I'm sorry I ever tagged you with that handle. That was UNSAT on my part. I deeply regret saying it. What are you going to do with the rest of your life?"

"There's a spiritual retreat camp further up the coast in Big Sur. I'll spend some time there living in a yurt. I'll soak in a redwood hot tub under the tall trees. It's where I can't see the sky. Perhaps that will cleanse my body and clear my head."

"I can come with you."

"No, you would make things more complicated. Besides, your friend Steve told me you need to take care of your bird, get her back into the air. The camp doesn't allow pets. I'll be in touch, sometime, maybe."

She stood up and walked away without looking back, his hand trailing empty. Soon, he heard the staccato bark of a Porsche six-cylinder engine fire up and the car depart. North from Ragged Point, the road follows the sawtooth coastline's ins and outs while maintaining a fixed level over the ocean like a high-water mark left by Noah's flood. Over the wind noise in the trees he followed the car's distinctive sound. It resembled ripping silk as it cycled through the gears. He listened as Melissa attacked the tortuous corners faster and faster until the mechanical scream faded, blocked by Big Sur's hills, and drowned out by the surf sounds below. There was nothing more to do but mount his own car and drive south.

Two hours later, the Corvette bounced across the rutted dirt parking lot beneath Morro Rock. On his way back south on the PCH, Frenchie spotted the Morro Bay exit and, on a whim, left the highway. He drove through the laid-back beach city and out to the rock towering over and defining the town.

His online research told him a pair of peregrines nested on the rock. He hoped to sight them. Parking the car down the beach, away from the people around the rock's base, he saw a group clustered around a tripod-mounted telescope. The half-dozen folks sported hiking boots, cargo shorts, sweatshirts, and shapeless cloth hats with wide brims. The "Granolas," as such folk are affectionally called locally, took turns looking through the lens pointed high on the rock. Frenchie ambled up to the birders and asked one;

"What's so interesting up there?"

The older chap replied, "A peregrine breeding pair always used that ledge as an aerie, but no one has seen the birds for weeks. We are wondering what happened to them and looking for signs they've been there. They're an endangered species and we would hate to lose them."

"Don't birds migrate? They might have gone south or north." Frenchie asked, feigning ignorance.

"Peregrines are very territorial. They claim a place and use it as a base camp for years. That's what worrying us about our pair gone missing."

Suddenly, he realized who his bird might be. Frenchie wished the group good luck and hurried back to the car before anyone looked in the passenger-side window. In the car, he saw her agitated and restless, moving back and forth across her perch and starring intently out the windshield toward Morro Rock. He had not the heart to leave her hood on during the drive. Flexed wings signaled an urge to fly. She knew where she was and she saw where she wanted to be.

Major decision points tended to come to Frenchie while in his car. To turn east to Louisiana or to emigrate west to California, he rolled the dice on that one. Now another choice loomed unexpectedly out of the blowing sea mist enveloping Morro Rock. He might hand the healing peregrine over to the birders. They would know where to take her for rehab. He felt sure no questions would be asked as to how he came to have her. Or, he could take her back to the winery hoping he could do right by her himself. If he gave her up, his life would once again be lonely and barren.

Yvette pranced out of his sight and Mousse drove north. Did he need the bird as much as she needed him? Healing can be a shared activity. It can begin over a glass of zinfandel, or several. It can occur while sharing bloody raw beef cubes. Maybe it could take place while alone, nude in a redwood hot tub. Unfortunately, sometimes broken wings, and souls, never mend. All one can do is try. Frenchie started the car and returned to the PCH.

Upon returning to the winery, on the plastic milk carton case serving as his front doorstep, he found two shiners, both marked with a bold "Z" in yellow wax pencil. One a Bordeaux bottle, the other Burgundy shaped; gifts and a subtle message from Steve.

Later that night in the trailer, he lay still; the room illuminated only by his phone's glow.

He sent a text to Yvette, "*Ravi de tu voir hier, tu étais formidable. J'espère que tout va bien.*" (Good to see you yesterday, you looked terrific. Hope all is well). He used only the familiar verb forms, the one for lovers and spouses.

Then one to Mousse, "Hope your drive north was fun. Keep in touch."

Before he nodded off, a reply text appeared from Yvette.

"*Merci, je l'ai apprécié. La prochaine fois, je porterai plus de vêtements, ou moins, ou pas de tout, ton choix.*" (Thanks, I enjoyed it. Next time, I'll wear more clothes, or less, or none. Your call). The return bounced back also couched in familiar verb forms.

Afterward, the phone remained silent and blank until it put itself to sleep and darkness took over the room.

In the twilight time between consciousness and sleep, between hard reality and distorted dreamland, he lay looking up at the trailer's wooden ceiling. The faded boards were hidden in the gloom. An image returned to him as it had so many times. The Iranian fighter plane exploded, blown apart by a Peregrine missile. Blazing, the wreckage tumbled end-over-end down to the Persian Gulf. No ejection seat, no parachute, ever emerged during the scene's replays in his head.

CHAPTER 25
BIG SUR, CALIFORNIA

Big Sur's 90-mile northward run is riven in many places by steep but shallow canyons drained by rocky streams. Resembling huge ravines more than proper canyons, the valleys penetrate like knife cuts a few hundred yards into the forested hills. Their precipitous sides and towering trees block any sight of the sea and obscure most of the sky. This is the land of majestic redwoods, massive Monterey pines, and truth-seeking humans escaping from what they consider to be an oppressive civilization. Hidden in these deep woods and by these pristine creeks live people scattered temporarily off the grid. Outsiders come here for enlightenment, self-awareness, and healing. All human activities in Big Sur are fueled by organic food.

The older woman pulled up a weather-beaten Adirondack chair, facing it toward where Melissa Taylor sat tapping her fingers on the arm of her own such chair. A low table in the resulting gap was resolutely removed, clearing any physical or symbolic barrier between them.

The joining woman showed the slender build and fit carriage of a dedicated hiker, her face shining with vibrant good health. She had a firm jaw, thin lips, soft eyes, fluid movements, and a PhD in psychology. Her age could have been 55, 65, or 75. It proved difficult for Melissa to guess how many years the woman possessed.

The counselor, she called herself a "Pathfinder," said she answered to "Ruth," a name she was quick to state was not on her birth certificate. It was one which seemed to her to be spiritual, biblical even. Her adopted handle was easy to remember and non-threatening. Evidently in the civilian domain it is not considered uncool to choose your own call sign. The senior female said nothing for a respectable length of time, then whispered with a knowing smile.

"So, Melissa, how are you coping without your phone?"

There is little cell coverage in most of Big Sur and none in the slit canyons. The camp barely featured running water and electricity. There was no WIFI, by design.

"Quite well, actually. Being out of contact has been a relief, not a pain," Melissa answered, returning a tight smile. "I didn't know I could cope without it."

"I'm told you need to talk to me, or someone like me. Where do you want to start? You'll find I'm a good listener."

Ruth leaned forward, giving Melissa the correct impression that the pathfinder listened intently.

Haltingly at first, but eventually the words and thoughts burst forth in a torrent. Over the next few afternoon hours, Melissa related her story. How her ambition to be a fighter squadron commander led her to giving in to sexual harassment and how it all blew up in her face. She held nothing back. All the dirty details spilled out, contaminating the campground's conifer-scented air. Ruth gently probed. With no personal knowledge of military affairs, she sought background information to understand the context of Melissa's situation.

"You say this dynamic began at the service academy. Isn't sexual exploitation common with immature people in secondary education?" Ruth asked, a neutral expression masking her face. If the sordid tale outraged her, she did not let her disgust show. Melissa went on.

"Yes, but when you're an 18-year-old freshman at the University of Texas and an upper classman comes on too strong, you can tell him to back off, push his hands away, or say, No! loudly. At the academy, senior-class students have military authority over juniors. They will make your life miserable with demerits, extra duties, or onerous assignments if you don't play the game."

"Do you want to tell me if you played the game?"

"Yes, I will and no, I didn't. Not until I graduated and got my pilot's wings, that's when the pressure grew more intense. Fighter squadrons are often manned by macho guys," Melissa said, stating the obvious. "Even then, the raunchy jokes, the sexual innuendos, the occasional come-ons were distasteful but bearable because I loved what I did, flying fighters."

"Didn't you tell me there is an outside organization responsible for investigating these sorts of problems?"

"Yes, it's the OSI. But they want concrete evidence, legal proof that will stand up in a legal hearing. The operatives, most are men, are good at investigating criminal matters. Not so much with she said—he said interactions. The actual problem is that it's the unit commander's responsibility for moral order and discipline in his unit."

Melissa put air quotes around "good order and discipline."

"Wing commanders are reluctant to probe situations like mine. They might reflect poorly on them, higher up the chain, on their leadership. When the sexual predator is a subordinate commander, there is even more incentive to cover things up"

"But you said this OSI organization got involved with the interplay, or the intercourse, between you and your commander."

"Yes, someone tipped them off on Conner's act. When the OSI came to interview me, to investigate, I told them the truth. That's when things got way tense."

Slowly, carefully, Melissa started treading the winding mental path to self-understanding. It is a trail of switchbacks and cul-de-sacs. She began to admit how her blind ambition put her at the mercy of an amoral monster. Tears fell on the dry forest floor in salty drips and the afternoon passed. Ruth continued to ask penetrating questions, leading her client without appearing to be in front. Her comments were non-judgmental but focused on what Melissa was feeling, both during the day's session and in the recent past. The light began to dawn, to illuminate the route to self-awareness, the light of insight into Melissa's inner motivations. The actual light in the camp did not correspond to the halting, tentative psychological brightness. Twilight fell suddenly in the ravine. Steep sides blocked the sun and shadows raced across the campground.

"Thank you for opening up to me, and to yourself. Can we meet here, same time, tomorrow?" Ruth asked.

"You know we have a group support session every night. Care to join in, have a glass of wine, or three, and share your story? *In Vino Veritas* " (in wine there is truth).

Melissa's demeanor changed. She flashed the look in her eyes Steve noticed, the one she was known for in her ex-squadron. Ruth leaned back in her chair. Her studied professional detachment failed her. The pathfinder shivered, but not from the deepening shadows. She probably had seen many things in her career, some terrible, some wonderful, but nothing like the fire in Melissa's eyes.

Overhead, still high in the fading sunlight, a red-tailed hawk called, "Scree! Scree!" The bird soared in the days' last thermals, wheeling, riding the updrafts for one last hunt before dark. Melissa starred up at the avian aviator and watched her glide and turn until the bird passed out of sight over the enveloping ridgeline.

"Tomorrow would be great, but tonight I'll pass, thank you. I am, or was, a single-seat fighter pilot. We fly alone. We fight alone. We even die alone," Melissa said.

Ruth too followed the hawk's soaring flight, then took a deep breath before speaking.

"You die alone? Don't we all?"

The pathfinder rose, leaving Melissa alone with her thoughts. The previous night, her first in the camp, she sat on the tiny deck outside her yurt, alone with a glass of wine. Motionless, she stayed until the sun disappeared into the unseen western sea and the cool darkness surrounded her. She felt comfortable in the early evening, hidden from her fellow campers, from the staff, from the world beyond Big Sur, and from herself.

In the black night of the soul ghosts are prone to appear. They materialized for her in the recent past. On other nights, she saw the specter of a smirking Bull

Conner, his carnal desire satiated at least for the moment. She pictured her gold-tinted oak leaf insignia, the mark of a major in the US Air Force. When night things got really bad, she often envisioned herself starring into a mirror and not recognizing the person looking back at her. Sometimes, she envisioned Frenchie with his outgoing Cajun charm replaced by an expression of surprised hurt when she hurled the words "prostitute" and "whore" back at him. That teary vision brought memories of the sensation of his hand between her thighs which in turn flooded her with the recall of how it felt to have him deep inside her. The longing was still there but had she burned her emotional bridges to him?

This night, after her first session with Ruth, none of those images came to her. For the time being, Big Sur's remoteness, the campground's isolation, and the catharsis of the conversation with the pathfinder was enough to keep the dire shades at bay. In the near distance, she could hear the ravine's foundation brook rushing toward the ocean. Melissa looked forward to a morning soak in a hot tub and to meeting Ruth again. She wondered if the first counseling session is always the hardest.

Chapter 26
Santa Rita Hills, California

The first sortie had been the hardest. The human attached a long lead, a strong string, to the jesses on her talons. They ventured out into a clearing in the vineyard. The falcon perched on his leather glove, gripping tightly. She flexed her wings, then gave a few exploratory flaps. Starling grape raiders, who once would have taken wing at the sight of her, remained interspersed among the fruit-laden vines. She had never flown while in their view. They collectively dismissed the potential threat. The man, with one sweep of his arm, launched her into the air. Instinctively she took tentative flight, exercising muscles stiff and weak from weeks of inactivity.

Flying for a falcon is analogous to bike riding for a human. Once mastered, the skill never atrophies, the muscle memory remains for life, however weakened by time are the muscles themselves. She staggered in the air, regained her stability, then circled over his head, her wings pumping air downward and rearward. The surprised starlings panicked, rising as one into a swirling dark cloud, leaving the vineyard en masse. After a few orbits 20 feet up, her wing strokes faltered. She tired. With gentle tugs on the string, he pulled her back to earth and to rest on his clenched, leather-armored fist. She folded her wings and squawked a cry of pure pleasure. Freedom was within her talons' grasp; she understood that. Her reward, a morsel of raw chicken from his belt pouch. After downing the treat in one gulp, she looked to the heavens from where she had just come. The sky waited for her. It always had and it always will for her and her kind.

Additional practice sorties continued in the dawn of each day and late in afternoons after the tasting room closed. Each sortie stretched longer in time and in distance covered. Bit by bit, her skill in the air returned, unlike the starlings who never came back. Frenchie was careful to limit her to orbits over vineyard areas not visible from the highway. No need to expose the forbidden bird to public eye and to possible notification to the Fish and Wildlife game wardens. The measure of food he provided in the field grew, until her diet consisted solely of rewards for successful flights, still on a lengthy line.

Once her endurance reached a level inspiring confidence, she could avoid a fatal collision with the ground, he deployed a lure to tempt her. Swung on end of a 10-foot cord, the lure mimicked a prey bird with fake feathers and a soft body. The peregrine recognized the faux fowl at once, attacking it in a shallow dive, a mini-stoop. Her reward, a tempting steak cube, very rare.

Soon came the day of the ultimate test. Would she, could she, return from a free flight, one without the confining tether? Frenchie looked forward to the airborne trial with mixed emotions. If the peregrine took wing and did not come back to his gloved hand, she would be gone, returning to where she belonged. Could she survive in the wild on her own? There was no way for him to predict predatory success against actual prey. She still knew how to hunt, but was her mended wing strong enough? The fused bone might have to withstand 15 Gs while pulling out of an extreme stoop.

If she returned from liberty, he would have his avian charge back and his rehabilitation mission would continue, at least for another day. The falcon's freedom became his raison d'être, his near-term goal in life. The tasting room, the wine, and his interaction with Steve passed the time, paid the bills, and kept the peace. Absent any contact with Mousse and not ready yet to pursue a rendezvous with Yvette, the peregrine falcon became Marcel Thibodeau's passion.

"You eventually must let her go, right?" Steve asked during an after-hours wine tasting session, the kind of meetings where friends speak their minds. Where Steve found it within himself to reveal his thoughts. "Her destiny's in the wild world she came from, not with you."

"I know, but not yet," Frenchie replied. Radically changing the subject, he asked, "Steve, have you ever killed anyone?"

Steve's jaw dropped. He stared intently at Frenchie; his eyes wide open. He took a deep breath and set his wineglass down with a splat, splashing the blood-red liquid on the bar of truth. *En vino veritas.*

"A few of my grape fermentations have gone horribly wrong, but I don't believe any tested toxic. No, I've never offed anybody. Have you?"

Steve posed the question Frenchie waited for and wanted to answer. Frenchie related in vivid detail his shoot-down of the Iranian jet, leaving nothing out. He ended with a description on how the burning plane's image haunted his dreams without respite night after night.

"It still bothers me. I have nightmares about the mission."

"Let me get this straight, Frenchie. You were under orders, as was the guy who got whacked, right? He would have done the same to you, correct? Sounds to me like a righteous hit."

Steve paused, choosing his words carefully, searching for something. His face lit up when he found it.

"There is usually a country and western song to fit any situation. Willie Nelson wrote a hit, *There's Nothing I Can Do About It Now.* My suggestion to you, my friend, is to move on."

Steve wiped 'the spilled red wine off the bar top with a flourish, threw the towel into the bin and left without further words.

***

One clear, cool morning he let her go. If she did not return, she would have all day to achieve a kill and feed off it. He removed her hood and untied the tether, leaving her jesses attached in case she came back. An upward thrust of his arm launched her into the early blue air and she took flight, circling overhead the vineyard counter-clockwise, free and unrestrained.

Frenchie watched her fly a few orbits, then swung the lure in a broad circle as high and fast as he could manage. The peregrine folded her wings into the classic swept-scimitar, low-drag position and dove from the sky to the stuffed toy. She missed-judged the intercept and zoomed upward, trading kinetic energy for height. He continued to whirl pretend prey, tempting her, urging her to re-attack. This time, she hit the target square, grasping it with both talons. Frenchie carefully drew it in. Close to him, she dropped the prize, flying to his fist, clutching his forearm, indenting his thick leather glove. Her reward was not the stuffed lure, but a sizeable chunk of beef. Salty tears watered the grapevines. Birds do not cry.

Midnight he lay in bed awake, barely keeping the re-occurring nightmare at bay. His phone pinged, announcing an incoming text. Not from Mousse. The message came from Yvette.

"Je serai à Santa Barbara lundi soir. Ca fait longtemps. Pouvons-nous nous réunir?" (I will be in Santa Barbara Monday night. It's been a long time. Can we get together?)

Frenchie took a deep breath, eyes wide open now, all drowsiness gone. Her message rang loud and clear. They would not be meeting to discuss books they read recently. He mulled the offer over and over, picturing the suggested sexual encounter. Yvette cheated on her husband with her boyfriend, now she burned to cheat on her boyfriend with her ex-husband.

Part of him reveled in the concept of carnal knowledge payback to the owner of the pickup truck she drove. He weighed the options. Revenge is a dish best served cold. Another, hotter part of him relished the promised illicit sex. Yvette was good in bed, enthusiastic and uninhibited. He remembered how her body enveloped his; her arms and legs wrapped in a tight embrace. How she took him inside her and kept him there until he fought for his breath like a newborn child. That mental image of her held considerable sex appeal. Was it the physical release he craved, or the stolen intimacy it involved? Who the hell knew? She would not expect an answer this late. He lived on a farm where folks slept early and woke with the dawn. Frenchie resolved to not dwell on that opportunity now. Could a relationship with his ex substitute for one with his falcon, which would soon end? He would think on it tomorrow. The bare bulb overhead was switched off. He fell back, perchance to sleep.

Just outside the trailer he heard an avian master of darkness, a great horned owl. Owls do not patrol the night sky, preferring to hunt from a high perch. Steve had erected several 30-foot, tee-topped poles at vineyard vantage points to attract owls as part of his all-natural rodent control program.

"Who? Who?" It is true. Owls ask that penetrating question, unseen in the night. Frenchie recalled the native people in the Louisiana swampland believed you can foresee your death by hearing an owl answer its own question by calling your name. But the silent flyers usually just ask the general question, "Who?" But what answer was the night stalker seeking? Who is Marcel Thibodeau? Who is Yvette? Who is Mousse? Who was the Persian pilot he killed? Are there owls in Iran and did the dead Iranian hear his name called out from the desert darkness?

Once again, Yvette's memory summoned old but vivid memories. The images came flooding back in a volcanic hot stream, the lava of desire. He saw her laying on her side in their Parisian hotel's fourposter bed. Light from the window, open to a view of the river Seine, played across her body. She wore nothing but red stiletto high heels. Jet-black hair fell askew, spread over a virgin-white pillow. One shapely leg, cocked just so, hid her lady parts. He remembered how smooth her skin felt under his touch. Later, the usual nightmare never arrived. His dreams were of a more unique and pleasurable sort.

CHAPTER 27
BIG SUR, CALIFORNIA

Melissa set off on foot early. The camp-furnished breakfast of free-range granola, organic fair-trade fruit, and biodynamic oat milk fostered an urge to escape in her. After leaving the retreat, she trekked east, deeper into the sheltering ravine cut into the saw tooth coastline. A dirt hiking trail led her to the old-growth redwood grove hidden deep in the mini-canyon. She soon found herself in the cool, dark forest. A crystalline brook draining from the precipitous watershed above showed her the way upstream, running along the path.

The morning's marine layer had not yet been burned off by the early dawn. Sea fog, dense and dripping with moisture, blanketed Big Sur north to south. Offshore in the night, the low shoal of clouds waited until morning to reclaim the land. It crept in like the Nothing in the movie *The Everlasting Story*. The rising sun warmed Big Sur's folded hills and generated rising thermals. The marine layer surged landward to fill the vacated airspace. It enveloped the shoreline and immersed the slopes' lower reaches in white mist, casting gray shadows everywhere. Easily at first, then more steeply, the track threaded her through massive redwood trees. Higher, their tops lost in the whiteness, their trunks shrouded in perpetual shadow even when there was no water vapor hiding the sun. The many-stepped journey gave her time to consider her next life-step. The isolation compelled her to think.

Her daily sessions with Ruth had become shorter, more to the point. No longer solely a sympathetic listener, the counselor/psychologist/pathfinder weighed in with gentle guidance. She offered focused, supportive encouragement. Ruth tried with limited success to dispel Melissa's deep sense of personal guilt and profound loss. The ex-pilot's mood became less dark. She began to wonder what the future might hold in store for her, if she could only grasp it.

Careful not to slip on the trail's dew-drenched rocks, she saw up ahead a brightening, a shining high in the fog layer. As she hiked upward, the redwoods and pines were becoming fewer, their trunks smaller in diameter. The dark underbrush gave way to a more open forestland. It was a landscape tipped on edge with vertical trees at an acute angle with the steep, sloping terrain. Finally, the trail became less precipitous. It thrust her from the thinning forest into a hilltop meadow. The plot presented a yellow riot of wild mustard blossoms, a pond of bright gold with banks of conifer green. Level now, the path ran along the razorback crest of the ridge she just climbed until it faded out on a cliff overlooking the fog-bound coast. She was above the marine blanket, above the fog, and in the bright sunlight of a mid-morning California day.

Catching her breath, she inhaled the view along with the cool air. Stretched beneath her lay the cloud bank, reaching to the horizon, an infinite field of cotton wool. Spectacular, but not an unfamiliar scene. Many flights in the F-16 had shown her what it was like to be above the weather, over the darkness, and in control. That was the key, wasn't it? To control yourself and to have agency over your status vis-à-vis others who may or may not have your best interests at heart. But first, you must know what you want traveling forward, whether at 500 mph or hiking speed. Ruth called the process "mindfulness." Inspired, Melissa reveled in the sight of the pristine white undercast obscuring a dreary world below her. She planned her reentry into that domain, much like piloting an aircraft and beginning an instrument letdown to a landing. This time, there was no radar controller to guide her, only a hired friend named Ruth.

Ruth told her, in her own non-threatening way, to consider the past to be just that, past. Ignore the dark behind or below, she counseled. The psychologist continued; mistakes often cannot be undone, but they can be overcome and learned from, particularly if your actions harmed no one other than yourself. Life goes on, a cliché which gained its exalted status by ringing useful and true.

Warmer in the sunshine and breathing easier after the climb, Melissa replayed her thoughts of the past few days like a recording from a mental thumb drive. Bull Conner pressured her into doing something she deeply regretted, making her feel cheap, venal, and used. Trading sex for advancement equals amateur prostitution. Frenchie was right as much as it hurt her to hear the word from him. Since the traumatic incident with Conner, the mere thought of sex made her nauseous. Whatever pleasure intercourse held before had evaporated. To Melissa, the physical act became a mentally detached business arrangement. Conner took that from her.

She could not blame the military system for what she did. Despite the dysfunctional U. S. Air Force legal process, there had been alternatives available to her. She should have gone to the OSI. But she did not. She could, however, fault the organization for fostering an environment where a predator like Conner could exist and even prosper. Mutual failures, the Air Force's and hers, is why she became a civilian, the first step to recovery. The Air Force lost a hot F-16 pilot, a future squadron commander, because of a warped value regime and an uncaring bureaucracy. A bureaucracy which put order above justice.

Life in the U. S. Air Force had been constraining, the system telling her where to live, what to wear, how to act, and placing her in harm's way. Like many armed service members, she traded away freedom of action on the ground for the opportunity to fly, to take to the limitless sky's wider, unbounded freedom however temporary until the fuel ran low. The struck bargain was simple. In payment for achieving her dreams of flight and command, she prepared to fight and perhaps to die, when her country asked. To cope with restricted military life was a key clause in the contract.

The other side of the bargain was the USA, through its military, would offer her safety and security on the earth. When her squadron commander violated his professional ethics and her body, the implied accord fell apart. Under pressure, she surrendered sexual self-respect in pursuit of promotion and of ultimate command, falling into Conner's trap. But that was then, this was now. After much thought, guided by Ruth, she vowed to trust her inner feelings more, to be mindful of what is right and what is wrong and to respond accordingly. Melissa now knew she needed to re-establish agency over her self in the future and to let the past be.

Obeying an urge welling up from deep inside, she slipped out of her clothes; a long logger's shirt, baggy jeans, muddy sneakers, undies. She arranged her things on the bare ground by the cliff's edge. She lay down on them, facing the sun and exposing her naked body to the cloudless sky. Relaxed for a change, she let old Sol's warm rays bathe her body.

The radiant void above she once ruled in a fighter jet seemed to melt the impurities out of her soul. Dross floated to the surface and dissipated. The raw sunlight felt far better than her daily soak in the lukewarm hot tub in a dark grotto of the redwood grove. Thinking hard, she dove deeply into herself, devising a plan. As she used to rehearse every aspect of a combat mission in her mind during the night before, she considered her future actions. Testing each contingency, each decision point, each back-up plan, and identifying all the key indicators, the plan came together. Once done, she gained peace with herself at last. It is never too late to enjoy a moral life.

Before the sun transitioned from a warming presence into a burning orb, she rose. Time to act like the rest of her life was about to begin. Standing nude on the rocky ledge, she saw the fog evaporating below her, revealing camp's tin roofs and scattered black yurts. Overhead, the local red-tailed hawk wheeled and glided, sunlight on its wings, hunting. Hawks, like falcons, are fanatically territorial. This had to be the same bird, or her mate, the one she and Ruth watched together. True soaring raptors, a red-tail masters the air effortlessly without needing to spend energy to stay aloft. The bird flew at peace with the sky and with itself.

The hawk, however obvious its expertise in flight, will always be a hawk, never an eagle nor a hummingbird. *That's the key, isn't it? To be able to change, to grow, to become something you are, at present, not,* Melissa thought to herself. Ever since adolescence, she pictured herself as a fighter pilot, nothing more, nothing less. It was fun while it lasted, but that phase of her life was complete. The persona of the fighter pilot is one of the most well-known and narrowly defined, professions in the world of work, no matter the nationality of the airplane driver. Few, if any, fighter jocks of either gender moonlight as interior decorators.

She found the new insight liberating. Now she could try to be whatever she wanted and do whatever her talents allowed. Time to take control of her life, to define for herself her own self-image. If there had been anyone around to observe, they would have easily recognized the look on Melissa's face, the look Steve noticed and which had given Ruth pause for reflection.

A fresh idea bubbled to the surface of her consciousness, one requiring immediate action. She pulled on and laced up her sneakers, then put on her long flannel shirt, carefully buttoned. She wore nothing else. If she stood up straight, did not bend over, and did not sit, the shirt would keep her modest, but only barely so. Along with her profession, along with her self-image, she now intended to control her sexuality. In the future she would be making consent decisions based on authentic emotions, not someone else's expectations and not through raw desire. With the rest of her clothes, Melissa

Taylor started back down the path intent on a new mission; Operation Self Respect. She meant to reclaim her passion, her agency, and just maybe, her lover.

Around noon and after a tearful farewell with Ruth, she departed the camp in her Porsche, headed south along the snake-track PCH. Not attacking the many curves and bends, a shear rock wall reaching up on her left, a deadly drop to the ocean on her right, she enjoyed driving the road more sedately. Instead of a frantic 9/10ths, as on her journey north, she let the fast car flow at a relaxed 7/10ths. It was a good day to drive the Pacific Coast Highway.

She stopped for an early sandwich; sprouts and avocado on whole wheat, at the Ragged Point Inn and, for the first time in days, turned on her phone. Several messages from Frenchie waited, including one with an extended embedded video of a peregrine falcon flying, his charge on the wing. She typed in, "The bird looks beautiful, when can I see her?" and hit send. That night, she shopped in San Luis Obispo, buying new jeans which fit like a second skin and a tight long-sleeve sweater with a turtleneck collar.

CHAPTER 28
SANTA RITA HILLS, CALIFORNIA

Each aerial sortie stretched longer, and she flew higher. The falcon became more proficient at attacking the whirling lure, rarely missing it. In the wild, her targets normally flew straight and level. If she managed a live intercept adroitly, her prey never saw her coming. The end game presented itself directly in front of her as a simple grab and go. If the intended meal sensed her approach and tried to evade her talons, only a slight change to her trajectory usually resulted in a quick kill. A circling lure challenged her flight skills. A pure pursuit path was never successful. If she attempted to a catch the fake bird from the rear, the spinning lure turned inside her flight path. She would miss, sliding to outside the circle. Thinking literally on the fly, she soon learned to aim across the circle and take the bait from inside its orbit. If she failed, a rare occurrence now, she could zoom into the vertical, reposition with a wing-over, and attack the lure once again across the 20' whirl. Each successful pounce on the target produced a reward from the human, either a bloody beef cube or a raw chicken nugget. Driven by hunger, blood lust, and habit, she adapted quickly. Her broken wing healed, but her mind did not. Her spirit, restless, did not relax in her new life.

By wild bird standards, she had it made. Plenty to eat, no competitors. No crows or eagles to avoid. She owned a safe place to roost, her mews. The human took care of her needs. As the days passed, she gained a grudging respect for the man, her man. "Affection" is too strong a word, and "dependence" is unfair. A raptor raised in captivity from eggdom to adulthood nearly always can be trusted to return to a falconer after a free flight. The bird would know no better or a freer life. But the peregrine tasted freedom in the wild, and she missed it. Each training and conditioning session, she flew further and further away before returning to take the whirling lure.

A peregrine can spot a small bird, real or fake, at well over a mile and a half. On most days, she never got that far from Frenchie, but she climbed until her silhouette shrank to but a dot in the vineyard's sky. From on high, she constantly chose the quickest path to a sure meal and clean mews in the trailer. Still, the wild called her stronger every day. Freedom waited for her impatiently out there in the endless blue.

***

Steve, his labors in the winery and vineyard paused for the day, rode his motorized quad up the vineyard hill to where Frenchie was flying the falcon. He rested on the small vehicle, watching nature's airshow. When the bird returned to Frenchie's armored glove, her meal devoured, and her leather hood safely in place, Steve spoke up.

"She's ready, isn't she? But are you prepared mentally to let her go? What you do with the bird is your decision, but we've pushed our luck with Fish and Wildlife. Not to mention the Sheriff, the FBI, and probably the CIA."

"Tomorrow's the day. I'll feed her well and take her to Morro Rock. Then she's on her own. I'm sure that's where she came from. I'll miss her."

"I know you will, but you need an actual life."

Back in the tasting room, Steve popped the cork on a bottle of a new sparkling wine he was working to develop. He poured Frenchie a flute bubbling full to celebrate the falcon's completed rehab. As the two friends watched sinuous lines of bubbles ascend in the trumpet-shaped wine glass, Steve regaled Frenchie with the terminology of Champagne, all words in French. The special bottle, the cork, the wire basket, the cork's metal cap, all had French names and all were unknown to Frenchie. Louisiana Cajun French pays no mind to sparkling wine. Frenchie's interest was piqued by the specific word describing the froth of bubbles floating on the golden liquid's surface. He asked Steve to spell that word, then spoke up.

"After the bird's release, I'll be gone all day tomorrow and tomorrow night. I'll be back in time to open on Tuesday."

"What's the big occasion? You'll let the falcon fly at dawn, then have the rest of the day free. I suspect there's a woman involved," Steve asked.

"I'm meeting Yvette in Santa Barbara. We have reservations at the best Cajun-Creole restaurant in town, the Palace Grill. I booked a night's stay at the Ritz-Carlton."

"Wow, I must pay you too much. My last question is, why?"

Frenchie took a healthy swig of the faux Champagne and looked at the ceiling, avoiding Steve's gaze. After a lengthy pause, he returned to face Steve, bubbles still rising in chained streams in his glass.

"Just horny, I guess. Maybe we can stick things back together. Maybe I'll buy a pickup truck. She seems to like them."

Steve inserted a temporary cork on the sparkling wine's green bottle, clamped it down, and replaced the shiner in the drink cooler under the bar. He stood up to leave the room, pausing to look back at his sole employee.

"Be sure that's what you want, my friend. Oh yeah, check this out. I made some calls. I did a little research."

Steve turned around and opened the tasting room's laptop, booting up a website. The title, in bold, was in Farsi, the language of Iran.

In the late 1970s, the Shah of Iran's regime self-destructed. Manipulative, corrupt Ayatollahs took over the Iranian government and began dictating to Persian society. A mass exodus of secular, well-to-do Persians emigrated, many to America. Rational, they wanted to avoid a stifling life ruled by a primitive theocracy.

Tens of thousands of Iranians settled into a welcoming Los Angeles. Their sophistication and business acumen allowed them to assimilate easily into American life. The expats, entrepreneurs all, established a vibrant local Persian culture, including a news website serving the Iranian diaspora. The site found by Steve included articles in English for second generation Persian-Americans whose Farsi was highly suspect.

Puzzled, Frenchie read the English subtitle, *Honor Killings on the Rise in Teheran.* Below lay a detailed story. The piece highlighted one notorious family in which male members were famous for executing female relatives deemed to have dishonored the extended family's name or besmirched its reputation. Death was the preferred clan punishment for deviant behavior, such as marrying for love or ditching their headscarves. One paragraph told how one youthful man of this fanatical family had been "martyred" in air combat with the forces of "The Great Satan" meaning America. His male relatives mourned his loss. Female members of his family remained silent.

"Sounds like this was your opponent. I told you it was a justified kill. The bastard had it coming. Now you might get some sleep," Steve said.

"How in hell did you find this?" Frenchie asked.

"I have a few close Persian friends from college at UC Davis. I made several calls. My buddies knew of this guy's family. Everyone knows everybody in upper-crust Persian society. They heard of him and pointed me to this website. They tell me that asshole whacked his own sister, strangled her with his bare hands. She had the nerve to kiss a non-related man in public. My Persian mates might mint a medal for you."

Steve, his information dump complete, folded the laptop dramatically, closing the book on Frenchie's MiG kill. He locked the tasting room door as the two friends left.

Frenchie turned in early to prepare for the momentous day and night ahead. Checking his phone, he saw two messages. Yvette texted, "Can't wait." The second came from Mousse, "The bird is gorgeous. When can I meet her? Sorry I've been comm out, but no cell phone reception in Big Sur."

Frenchie returned Mousse's message. "Meet me in the parking lot at the base of Morro Rock in Morro Bay at 0600 tomorrow. It's Freedom Day."

The text from Mousse appeared as a shock to Frenchie. Labeling a woman a "prostitute" when "victim" would be more accurate is not often a path leading to romantic bliss. He could say a last goodbye to the peregrine and Mousse at the same time. With those two disparate females out of his life, maybe an intimate dinner followed by a roll in the hay with Yvette would reduce his stress level enough for him to plan his future. Maybe he could re-establish a solid relationship with his ex. Maybe the moon would fall from the sky.

Later, the nightmare returned, only updated. The image of the burning fighter aircraft faded away. A notional banner on the Farsi news website replaced it. *NO 72 VIRGINS!* screamed the headline. The subtitle read, *Martyred Honor Killer, to His Very Great Surprise, Finds Himself in Hell.*

CHAPTER 29
MORRO BAY, CALIFORNIA

An early morning offshore breeze, known locally as the Santa Lucia Wind, pushed the marine layer, the Nothing, far out to sea, near the hazy horizon. The zephyr left the Central Coast crystalline and cool from Vandenberg Space Base north to the far reaches of Big Sur and Monterrey, California. The sky's intensity, only a half-hour after dawn's first glimmers, burned with a cobalt blue seldom enjoyed along the often foggy shoreline.

They met beside his Corvette after her Porsche pulled up next to it in the expansive, deserted parking lot. From an arm's length apart, Frenchie could not help but admire her slim figure displayed in sprayed-on jeans and a tight sweater. He had only seen her in shapeless flight suits, baggy clothes, and completely nude. Impressed, he spoke first.

"Good morning, Mousse, check that, I mean Melissa."

"That's OK, I still sometimes think of myself as Mousse. How have you been, Marcel?"

The question carried more than the usual common pleasantry. She drew out the words slowly, then paused for a breath of fresh sea air, looking into his eyes.

"Not bad. Today's the day the peregrine leaves me for her aerie, up there on the rock. It's hard to let go of something, or someone, you care for, but she needs her freedom."

"Can I hold the bird before she takes flight? I was a falconer for four years, with the official mascots at the Air Force Academy. We free-flew our birds over the stadium crowd at every home football game."

"Yikes, Melissa. I had no idea. You could have helped me with her. At LSU, our mascot was a Bengal tiger. We didn't let him go into the stands at games."

Frenchie handed her the leather glove and opened the Corvette's passenger-side door. The falcon anxiously skated back and forth on her perch, peering up at Morro Rock and flexing her wings in anticipation. Melissa expertly and gently removed the bird from the car, holding tight to the jesses. Still starring at the massive cliffs, the peregrine settled down a bit, grasping Melissa's leather-armored arm.

"Do you have any food for her? She needs to eat before flying."

From his leather treat bag, Frenchie handed Melissa three large cubes of raw filet mignon, the most expensive beef he could find in the base commissary. Melissa fed two morsels to the bird, who wolfed both down straightaway. The third she ate herself. Frenchie finished the final meat morsel remaining in the pouch, chewing, and watching the bird, his peregrine, on Melissa's arm. He realized those two females ranked even more important to him than he had ever considered.

194

Melissa could pet the bird, stroking her crop below that hooked beak with the back of her fingers. something Frenchie had never been allowed to do. Whenever he tried to pet the top or back of the falcon's head, she objected strenuously. That vital region is the kill zone, where fatal thrusts originate, not affection.

"At the Blue Zoo, the academy, we never released a falcon into the wild. It broke my heart knowing none would ever fly free. I dreamed of letting them all go, but I never did, not even one. This is a special day for you and for her. Thanks for sharing it with me."

A few early risers, joggers, and beach walkers gathered around the two sports cars, attracted by the bird's flexing, flapping wings.

"She suffered a broken wing. It's healed now, and strong. She remembers how to use it," Frenchie said, to no one in particular, but focused on his ex-squadron mate.

"Was it hard for her to recover?" Melissa asked.

"Yes, she had to fight through crippling pain. She came back, all the way back, stronger than ever, ready to take on the world, confident and secure."

"We're talking about more than the bird, aren't we?"

"That's for you to decide, Melissa. I suppose it's time for her freedom, if she wants it."

He untied the jesses from her talons. As soon as she sensed her legs unbound, the peregrine launched herself into the sky, leaving Melissa's arm, her wings stroking the air, free at last.

"Godspeed, good luck, and good hunting." It was all Frenchie could get out, a catch in his throat.

The climbing bird circled the small group of humans below, rising higher and higher into the cool dawn air. After several orbits at altitude, she folded her wings into the low-drag stoop position and pointed her beak down at the upturned pale faces watching her from below. Hurtling earthward at well over 100 mph, she plunged, pulling out of the dive not 10 feet overhead. She used the kinetic energy gained in the stoop to soar upward once again, picked up one more circle over the people, and flew off toward nearby Morro Rock. Flocks of resident shorebirds took flight in panic. Used to being unmolested and un-preyed upon from the air. It alarmed them to see the falcon, their nemesis, return. Soon, she disappeared from sight, into the sky.

"She's saying goodbye," Melissa whispered, her voice cracking, barely audible over the distant surf.

"That or looking for the lure I used to call her. I'll go with your interpretation."

Frenchie took a deep breath and wiped his face with the back of his sleeve. He threw the unneeded leather glove and dangling, empty jesses into the car, while fumbling for his keys.

"It's a delightful morning, let's go for a walk on the beach, Marcel," Melissa said.

From Morro Rock the broad, flat beach stretches north for five miles to the quirky beach town of Cayucos. The empty expanse is devoid of structures or interruptions. It is deserted early in the day. The hard-packed wet sand near the water made for easy walking, with the roiling, crashing surf on one side of the strolling pair and soft, white powder on the other. Overhead, unseen but not unheard, jet fighters rumbled like the mutter of distant thunder. Melissa looked up for the source of the rolling noise, and stared east, into the sun, shading her face with her hand.

"It's the dawn patrol; F-18 Hornets from the US Navy. We're under one of their air combat practice areas. Those guys and gals up there are enjoying the most fun you can have with your clothes on," he said.

"Until they have to go out and land those airplanes on a boat. At night."

"Well, yeah, there's that. Do you miss it, Mousse, the flying?"

He had trouble thinking of the woman beside him in the context of aviation without using the call sign she had disavowed.

"Not really. Once I resigned my commission, I decided not to, to look forward, not back. I do miss being in a fighter squadron though, with our squadron mates. A few I miss more than others. How's about you, Frenchie?"

"Yeah, I miss it, flying with the mates. But I'll miss the bird more. That's a hell of note, isn't it?"

The two ex-pilots walked on silently. The jet rumble faded away, replaced by the softer cries of resident shorebirds. Sometimes, things are said without thinking, without calculation, without artifice. These are the thoughts coming directly from the heart. Too often they go unsaid, but when spoken, the effect can be profound on both the speaker and the listener.

"I really miss flying with you, Mousse, sorry, Melissa. I miss our pool games. I miss you."

She reached out and took his hand. Their fingers intertwined, they walked on in silence. A 100 yards farther down the empty strand, Melissa spoke up. He struggled to hear her over the pounding surf.

"You went to the OSI, didn't you?"

"Yeah, I did."

There was little he could add to the simple admission of his action. He thought anything additional would make matters worse.

"Thank you," she replied. There was nothing else to say."

"Speaking of people we don't miss, whatever happened to our ex-commander?" Frenchie asked.

He instantly regretted bringing up what had to be a painful subject for the woman holding tight to his hand. But again, some thoughts need to be expressed and some questions must be asked. "He got shoved out of the Air Force on a 'bad paper' discharge with no pension. She put "bad paper" in air quotes with her free hand. Last I heard, he's managing a convenience store somewhere in Texas. The system finally worked, thanks to you getting involved, uninvited."

"Where in Texas, Purgatory?"

"No, that town's in the Hill Country. Our ex-fearless leader hails from East Texas." Melissa cleared things up.

"Yeah, he did mention that in passing once."

"Gone, now it's his time to be forgotten. Done." Frenchie went on. "My friend, winemaker Steve, educated me on the nomenclature of champagne. When bubbles rise in a glass, driven by effervescence, they float on top. It's a sign the wine is alive, engaging, and mature. That layer is called the "mousse" and is an indication of high quality and vivid life."

Frenchie surprised even himself with his unexpected articulateness.

Again, there was nothing to say. Nothing to add. By unstated mutual agreement, or perhaps by subliminal desire, they turned to face each other. The low sun behind her lit up her blonde locks and highlighted her figure, revealing much more than the chow hall's harsh light back in the desert. He had her tight jeans and snug top to thank for the improved viewing. Yellow sunlight played with her hair, blowing in the gusty wind, obscuring her face but illuminating her womanhood. The sun made it difficult to see her. Frenchie parted the wispy strands hiding her face with both hands, revealing the tracks of her tears streaming down her wind-kissed cheeks. He let his fingertips trail down her jaw, raising her face up to his.

Sometimes a kiss is a greeting, an air kiss, sometimes a kiss expresses fond affection, or makes a statement of burning desire. Sometimes it is much, much more than all of these. This was one of those last-named times. As he held her tight and their lips met, she moved his hands from around her narrow waist sliding down to her flaring buns. His cupped fingers found the folds of her cheeks through her skin-tight jeans and he felt the sunlight on his closed eyes. Was the salt he tasted from the sea breeze, did it come from her tears, or from his? After a lifetime kiss, he wrapped his arms around her and stoked her hair. She rested her head on his shoulders. Frenchie spoke first.

"Shouldn't we be rolling around in the surf like Burt Lancaster and Deborah Kerr in *From Here to Eternity?*"

"What are you, nuts? That scene took place in Hawaii. The North Pacific Ocean here would freeze our butts off," Melissa said.

Finally, they turned and started back to where the cars waited, walking again in silence. She spoke up in a tone of voice he had never heard from her, but had always wanted to. She had that look in her eyes.

"I have a room in a charming boutique hotel on the Embarcadero here in Morro Bay, the Estero Inn. The manager says I can bring in one guest. I nominate you."

Without looking toward her, Frenchie replied, "Let's get breakfast first, there's a coffee shop, the Sun and Buns, on the waterfront. We're in no hurry, and I have a notion we'll have a long time together. I'll meet you there. I have a meeting in Santa Barbara to cancel."

CHAPTER 30
MORRO BAY, CALIFORNIA

Her wings, strong and flexible once again, drove her skyward. She fought the offshore wind, blowing stronger at altitude, tried to drive her out to sea. The peregrine circled the scene far below her, keeping a watchful eye on her human companion. Another human had joined him, this one smaller with yellow fur on her head. That was the one who launched the bird into her realm of the sky, free at last. The falcon hesitated for a few moments, waiting to spot a whirling lure. That would signal an opportunity for a practice kill and a quick snack, but no lure appeared. All she could see were upturned pale faces. A small crowd had gathered to watch her fly. Her surveillance of the humans on the strand below bordered on lackadaisical as her attention soon diverted to where she was, home. Her aerie on Morro Rock waited for her return. She felt torn between flying to it and continuing to orbit over the parking lot.

At last she decided, but not without one last pass. Apex predators, the ultimate killing machines, do not waste energy on trivial pursuits, almost never play, and are usually,totally dedicated to their bloody business. But even so, sometimes the freedom of unrestricted flight sparks what humans perceive as a joyous flight maneuver with no obvious survival purpose. She felt the need, the need for speed. Her wings folded into the classic teardrop profile, she let her head fall far below the horizon. The peregrine pointed vertically toward the group of humans gathered beside the two sports cars. One human had been her savior, her protector, and her trainer. Another one was the unknown new freedom friend.

Diving downhill, her airspeed picked up rapidly, 60 mph, 80 mph, 100 mph, and more. She started her recovery pullout 100 feet over the ground, pulling ten Gs. Her mended wing held the strain without pain. Screaming overhead past the upturned faces at 75 mph, she saw both her humans showing their teeth in smiles. She zoomed upward, trading airspeed for altitude, adding an occasional wing thrust. Quickly, she found an updraft where the Santa Lucia Wind struck Morro Rock's vertical shoreward face. She allowed it to hurl her into the cloudless sky without looking back. It was a good day, check that, it was a great day to be a peregrine falcon.

THE END

ACKNOWLEDGMENTS

The following helpful people provided valuable information and insight in the writing of this book. My heartfelt thanks to all.

Heidi Cobleigh

Carolyn Berndt

Lisa Fisher

Pat Kempton

Dr. Sharon Murphy

Dr. Ben Lambeth

Lt. Col. Ed Petersen

Jean Petersen

Jeff Koligian

Lt. Col. Kirk Huhta

Mindy T. Conde

Natalie McDermott

ABOUT THE AUTHOR

Ed Cobleigh flew 375 combat missions in the F-4 Phantom, earning two Distinguished Flying Crosses and the Air Medal. He has flown fighter planes with the US Air Force, the US Navy, the Royal Air Force, the French Air Force, and the Imperial Iranian Air Force. His log book shows time in the F-104 Starfighter, F-4 Phantom, A-4 Skyhawk, GR1/T2 Anglo-French Jaguar, and the F-16 Viper. As an instructor, he taught student pilots at the U. S. Air Force Fighter Weapons School, the USN Fighter Weapons School (Top Gun), and the RAF Qualified Weapons Instructor Course (Jaguar). He co-authored the U. S. Air Force air-to-air tactics manual.

Serving as an Air Intelligence Officer, he worked with the CIA, FBI, and MI6 on a variety of classified intelligence projects. He is proficient at ferreting out information and connecting dots others may have missed. Ed has visited 50 countries in various capacities and has lived in Scotland and Thailand. He knows Paris well, traveling there over 50 times.

His memoir, *War for the Hell of It: A Fighter Pilot's View of Vietnam*, was a #1 Amazon bestseller. *The Pilot: Fighter Planes and Paris*, his literary aviation novel, gained excellent reviews and has sold well. *The First Fighter Pilot-Roland Garros: The Life and Times of the Playboy Who Invented Air Combat*, by Ed, was named the best new biography on WWI. He has been on the faculty of the Central Coast Writers Conference and his op/ed pieces on fighter weapons and tactics have been published in numerous journals and magazines. Cobleigh has sold over 26,000 books in 12 countries in three genres and two languages.

Ed Cobleigh and his wife, Heidi, live in California's wine country with their dogs and horses.

BOOK REVIEWS

Readers are invited, requested even, to post a review on this book's home page at www.Amazon.com. Reviews need not be lengthy, but they should be honest accounts of how the reader perceived the book, the highs and the lows, the good, the bad, and the ugly. Reviews will allow prospective buyers to make an informed decision.

Thanks in Advance;
Lt. Col. Ed Cobleigh U. S. Air Force (Retired)
Fighter Pilot.
Call sign, "Fast Eddie"

ALSO BY ED COBLEIGH
www.EdCobleigh.com

Fighter Planes and Paris
The Pilot

An aviation/adventure novel.

The Pilot loves fighter planes, a beautiful woman, and Paris, but can only have one of the three. His problem is a beautiful, mysterious French woman who may be a spy. Why does she keep haunting his memories? In making his difficult choice, the Pilot remembers classic combat missions from WWI to Desert Storm while re-living past love affairs, but who were they with? Fast-paced in the City of Light, *The Pilot: Fighter Planes and Paris* delivers a tale of passion, air combat, and history. You are in the cockpit, in the bedroom, in Paris, looking to answer the questions, "Who is the Pilot?" and "Who is his Parisian lover?"

A Fighter Pilot's View of Vietnam
War for the Hell of It

A deeply personal account of a fighter pilot's life and his journey into airborne hell and back.

Ed, "Fast Eddie," Cobleigh served two tours of duty during the Vietnam air war, logging 375 combat sorties in the F-4 Phantom fighter/bomber. In *War for the Hell of It*, Cobleigh shares his perspectives in a deeply personal account of a fighter pilot's life, one filled with moral ambiguity and military absurdities offset by the undeniable thrill of flying a fighter aircraft. This is an unprecedented look into the state of mind of a pilot as he experiences everything from the carnage of a crash to the joy of flying through a star-studded night sky, from the illogical political agendas of Washington to his own dangerous addiction to risk. Cobleigh gives a stirring and emotional description of one man's journey into airborne hell and back, recounting the pleasures and the pain. the wins and the losses. and ultimately, the return.

The First Fighter Pilot
Roland Garros
Life and times of the Playboy Who Invented Air Combat

In the Spring of 1915, a Parisian playboy took to the lethal skies of World War I, becoming the world's first fighter pilot. Never before had a lone pilot hunted down other aviators. Roland Garros' aerial exploits unleashed unlimited air combat and changed warfare forever.

Before leaving French café society for the Western Front, the young pilot set aviation records, won air races, and introduced manned flight to thrilled crowds in the USA, Europe, and Latin America. In combat, he was shot down, escaped, and made his way back to the waiting arms of an exotic dancer. His decision-stay in Paris or return to the front lines. Garros needed two more victories to become an ace. The little-known story of Roland Garros' exciting life and his fascinating times is a riveting tale well worth the telling. Learn how a pioneer pilot of the Gilded Age descended into the man-made hell of the Great War. This narrative non-fiction biography delivers that stirring account right on target.